ONE
MAN
SHOW

Titles by Michael Innes:

APPLEBY ON ARARAT

THE BLOODY WOOD

THE CASE OF THE JOURNEYING BOY

THE CRABTREE AFFAIR

DEATH BY WATER

DEATH ON A QUIET DAY

HARE SITTING UP

THE LONG FAREWELL

THE MAN FROM THE SEA

ONE MAN SHOW

THE SECRET VANGUARD

THE WEIGHT OF THE EVIDENCE

ONE
MAN
SHOW

Michael Innes

HarperPerennial
A Division of HarperCollinsPublishers

A hardcover edition of this book was originally published in 1952 by Dodd, Mead & Company and was published in England under the title *A Private View*. It is here reprinted by arrangement.

First Perennial Library edition published 1983. First Harper-Perennial edition published 1991.

ISBN 0-06-080672-9
91 92 93 94 95 WB/OPM 10 9 8 7 6 5 4 3 2 1

ONE
MAN
SHOW

1

Lady Appleby finished her coffee, drew on her gloves and glanced round the restaurant. "John," she asked her husband, "did you say you needn't be back at the Yard till three o'clock?"

"I believe I did." Sir John Appleby called for his bill. "Was it rash of me? Are you going to take me for an hour's quick shopping?"

"Of course not. All men hate shopping. But it means we've just time to go to the Da Vinci. There's a new show."

"Has it ever occurred to you that perhaps all men hate new shows? And with you, Judith, new shows *are* shopping, as often as not. The number of paintings you've bought in the course of the last year——"

"You know that all my carvings now *need* paintings as backgrounds." Judith Appleby was a sculptress by profession. "And at the moment I very much want something abstract, with strong diagonals, and plenty of acid greens."

"It's ridiculous to buy modern paintings virtually as wallpaper."

"Nonsense. It's just what they should be bought for."

"And the sort of price you seem prepared——"

"Very well. We won't go. No doubt I've been spending too much on that sort of thing. I shall go to a cinema."

"Come along." Appleby dropped a florin on the plate before him and rose. "But I make one condition. We conduct this matter in a businesslike way. As soon as we've paid our shillings——"

"But, John, there won't be *anything* to pay . . . not to get in, I mean. It's the private view, and I've had a card." Judith contrived to present this as a factor of considerable financial significance.

"Very well. As soon as we are inside I shall send for Mr Da Vinci——"

"His name's Brown."

"I shall send for Mr Brown and address him in this way. 'My wife,' I shall say, 'requires a good quality picture, about three feet by four, with strong diagonals, and in the new season's acid greens. Will you be good enough to show us anything you have in stock?'"

"Brown would find that very offensive. He has no sense of humour—or certainly not of English schoolboy humour. You'd better keep quiet until the bargaining. Then you can come in for all you're worth."

"Thank you very much." Appleby fed his wife briskly through a revolving door and joined her on the pavement. "Are you sure you'll find diagonals and things at this particular show?"

"Pretty sure. It's an exhibition of painting by——"

Judith checked herself. "Hadn't we better take a taxi? Because of your appointment at three. But I'll pay."

They climbed into a taxi in silence. Once settled in it, Appleby favoured his wife with a glance of frank domestic suspicion. "What sort of a private view?" he asked. "One of the kind with an opening ceremony and a pretentious speech?"

"Certainly—a speech by Mervyn Twist. But that will probably be over by the time we get there. We'll just look round and come away. I don't expect there will really be anything worth thinking of." Judith was soothing.

"Very well." Her husband sank back in the taxi, resigned. "Where is this Da Vinci? We don't seem to be going in the direction of the very grand places of that sort. Here's Charing Cross Road."

"Brown—his real name is Hildebert Braunkopf— hasn't been going very long. This show's important to him."

Again mild suspicion rose in Appleby. "Will the painter be hanging round? Will he be some poor devil one feels one must in decency ask to a square meal? Remember the man who took your spoons last summer."

Judith shook her head. "Politic worms."

"What's that you say?"

"A certain convocation of politic worms are e'en at him. It's a memorial exhibition. This painter's dead."

With a deplorable access of good humour, Appleby felt in his pocket for change. "But sometimes there's a sister who does something herself. Or a sorrowing and inebriated father earning penurious bread as a drawing-master in Bootle."

"I don't think there will be anybody of that sort

3

either. It's a memorial exhibition of the work of Gavin Limbert."

Appleby sat up with a jerk. "Really, Judith, this is too bad."

Judith Appleby looked at her husband with the largest reasonableness and innocence. "I don't see why we should have to keep away from the poor man's pictures just because he was murdered."

"Found shot. It happened while I was abroad. But I gather it isn't at all known that he was murdered."

They had come to a halt, and Appleby gloomily made the harassing calculations necessary before paying a London taxi-driver in the year 1951. He peered out as he did so—whereupon an observant constable stepped smartly forward, opened the door and saluted. An equally observant press photographer snapped this up in a flash. It was a gratifying moment for the small crowd gathered to gape at the undistinguished façade of the Da Vinci, and they now turned to gape at the Applebys instead. Appleby, who would have liked to scowl furiously at his wife, contented himself with scowling furiously at these idlers. This at once gave the impression of his representing the full severity of the law, hot-footed in pursuit of crime. A second constable, for whom the appearance of an Assistant Commissioner constituted an event of decisive professional importance, threw himself happily into the task of further dramatising the occasion by clearing a path as if for the arrival of an archbishop or a cabinet minister. From the window of the Da Vinci, which was handsomely draped in very new and very sombre purple velvet, a large stone Buddha surveyed this scene with detached and ironic satisfaction. Judith, who appeared unaware of anything out of the way in their arrival, paused to give this seemingly ancient object a critical glance. "*Atelier Braunkopf*," she said. "I expect he carves them in the basement, mostly out of old tombstones. Clever little man."

"But there's a label on it saying 'Fourth Century.' He should be put in gaol."

"He'd say that the statue was warranted only as illustrative of the art of that period, and not as representing it. By the way, if we do buy anything, remember he will want two cheques."

"Two cheques?" Appleby paused with his hand on the door of the Da Vinci. "You mean he expects things paid for twice over?"

"Of course not. Braunkopf just likes two cheques— each for one half of the amount. I can't think why. Might it be something to do with income tax?"

Appleby breathed rather hard. "I think it just conceivable that it might."

"Would it make it quite legal if I gave him the one cheque and you gave him the other?"

"When you are in this mood, my dear, it is useless to talk to you. . . . Was that Gavin Limbert?"

On the inner side of the glass door before them was displayed a photograph of a youth perhaps twenty-three years old. He was untidily dressed in what could be distinguished as very good clothes; he sat on a soap-box amid a litter of painter's materials; he looked extremely happy and wholesome and innocent. A thoroughly nice public schoolboy, Appleby thought, trying himself out in a rôle that had taken his fancy, and blessed with a father or an aunt willing to put up four or five hundred a year for the duration of the experiment. It was hard to imagine a sinister or even a shady side to the life of Gavin Limbert. But one

5

never knew. . . . Appleby let his eye travel from the photograph to an announcement displayed beneath it:

GAVIN LIMBERT
MEMORIAL EXHIBITION
OILS
GOUACHES
COLLAGES
TROUVAILLES

"I know about *gouaches* and *collages*," he said. "But what are *trouvailles*?"

"That will be things he picked up on the sea-shore— old bits of cork, and nicely eroded stones." Judith was fishing from her bag the card that was to admit them to a view of these interesting objects. "A sort of aesthetic beachcombing."

"And people will *buy* them?" Appleby pushed open the door.

"Yes. They pay for the artist's eye. . . . It's terribly respectable."

The outer room of the Da Vinci Gallery was certainly making a bold bid to suggest older-established institutions of its own kind off Bond Street. The walls were hung with dim and darkened pictures, bearing labels which for the most part took the form of honest doubts and frank disclaimers. Mr Brown, indeed, had so far improved upon the accepted convention in these matters as to indicate the degree of his establishment's dubiety over its treasures by a system of multiple question-marks. "*Studio of Rubens?*" Appleby read. "*Possibly by a pupil of Dirck Hals??*" "*Formerly attributed to Rembrandt: rejected by Borenius.*" "*El Greco????*" "*Perhaps Alessio Baldovinetti: not ac-*

6

cepted by Berenson." One or two of the pictures were simply labelled "?" or "???" Anyone wishing to linger amid this orgy of scepticism could do so upon settees massively upholstered in red plush.

But Judith Appleby pressed on. "Brown's not hoping to sell this stuff," she explained. "He's just borrowed it from some of his pals. It reminds the customers that Gavin Limbert may be an Alessio Baldovinetti one day."

"I suspect Alessio did it without going to the trouble of being found mysteriously dead. . . . Look out." Appleby drew his wife aside just in time to prevent her being bowled over by a complex object being propelled on wheels from a farther room. "Whatever is that?"

"Television, I think. And I saw a van with newsreel people outside. Glory for Brown."

"And for Limbert, I suppose. Shall we really push in? There's a terrific crush. And I think the beastly opening is still happening."

Judith nodded. "It certainly is. I can hear Mervyn Twist's voice. Come on."

She insinuated herself through a narrow gap between two massive women. With rather more difficulty, and with much less enthusiasm, Appleby followed. He frowned as he saw a young man from an evening paper making a quick note of his name, and then took a glance round the crowded room. The only pictures available to his inspection were those along the wall by which he stood, and his position was such that they appeared in a drastic foreshortening. But if their proportions were thus obscured, their general character was plain, and it was evident that Limbert had been an abstract painter. Or, more strictly, it was

7

evident that he had given himself to producing abstract paintings. For Appleby doubted whether this amiable and unfortunate young man had possessed a temperament very congruous with any convinced turning away from the natural world. Most of the paintings were conscientiously flat and two dimensional; and where they admitted of a third dimension they did so only in the rarefied spirit of Sixth Form geometry. But lurking in them were things known outside either the studio or the class-room. The pure ellipses could be felt as yearning after the condition of Rugby footballs; and slanting across several of the canvases was a diminishing series of white rectangles from which Appleby was disposed to infer that at one time a principal ambition of young Limbert's had been winning the under-fifteen hurdles. Moreover the paintings were obstinately atmospheric. The light which played upon them came from a real world— from one in which sunshine sifts through green boughs or strikes up from clear water. They hinted at a more catholic enjoyment of created things than they were prepared openly to admit. Appleby felt obscurely that here had been a promising young man, although not perhaps a promising young painter. And it was not at all clear why he should be dead—unless, indeed, he had been butchered to make Mr Hildebert Brown or Braunkopf this highly remunerative holiday. Appleby promised himself to send for the officer dealing with the Limbert affair and discover what progress had been made with it.

The gallery was crowded—presumably with persons interested in the progress of the arts. Half of them were seated on several rows of chairs facing the farther wall; a few had been accommodated, after the fashion of a platform party, with rather grander chairs facing the other way; the remainder were standing in a huddle about the room. Appleby, whose business had for long been the observation of human behaviour, saw that while all had the appearance of following Mervyn Twist, a large majority was in fact exclusively concerned with disposing and maintaining the facial muscles in lines suggestive of superior critical discrimination. Some put their faith in raised eyebrows, thereby indicating that while they approved of the speaker's line as a whole, they were nevertheless obliged, in consequence of their own fuller knowledge, to deprecate aspects of it. Others had perfected a hovering smile, indicative of discreet participation in some hidden significance of the words. Yet others contented themselves with looking extremely wooden, as if conscious that the preserving of a poker face was the only safe and civil way of receiving observations which their uninhibited judgment would be obliged to greet with ridicule. Appleby found the spectacle depressing. Gavin Limbert had perhaps been lucky, after all. He had died young and untouched by disillusion—ignorant or careless of the oceans of twaddle and humbug which constitute the main response of the Anglo-Saxon peoples to any form of artistic expression.

But now Mervyn Twist appeared to be approaching his peroration. He was a youngish man, with an indeterminate face suggestive of an under-exposed photographic plate, and a high, screaming voice. If one listened for long enough, Appleby supposed, some semblance of intelligible utterance, some rough approximation to the divine gift of discursive speech, might piece itself together amid these horrible noises.

9

As it was, nothing reached him but a mush of arbitrarily associated words. *The heroic era of the first papiers collés . . . golden sunset of the fruit-dish, the bottle and the guitar . . . his second and third ego wrestling with the demon . . . magnificent proportions of Teotihuacan . . . correspondence to a sublime internal necessity. . . .* With sudden marked discomfort Appleby realised that he had himself assumed a very wooden expression indeed. He was just wondering what he could possibly substitute instead—self-consciousness is extremely infectious—when Twist suddenly stopped speaking and sat down. There was a polite ripple of applause. Somebody whom it was impossible to see got up and moved a vote of thanks. But nobody paid much attention to this. The company began milling round the pictures.

"I thought we'd better have one of these." Judith had disappeared into the crowd and now returned carrying a catalogue.

"Was it free?"

"Free to me. But it means that Braunkopf spotted me and is coming over to be introduced to you. I expect he'll want to show us round himself."

Appleby took the catalogue in deepening gloom. The outside bore the inscription: "G. L.: 1928–1951." Below this was an engraving of a pair of compasses, with one foot broken off short in the act of describing an incomplete circle. "In excellent taste," Judith said. "And finely allusive. 'On earth the broken arc, in heaven the perfect round'. And there's another nice Braunkopf touch over there where Twist was speaking from."

It occurred to Appleby that he was coming to find Judith in this particular vein of ironic connoisseurship

10

increasingly baffling. He must be ageing more rapidly than she was. He looked across the room and saw that Twist had been posed before a painting larger than the rest and somewhat different in character. Above this the presiding genius of the Da Vinci had caused to be suspended a palette surrounded by a laurel wreath and enriched with a big black crepe bow.

"Dash it all, Judith, the man was *alive*, you know—and an artist just like yourself. Not ten days ago he was waking up, and cooking his breakfast, and planning the day's work. Now he has this beastly little dealer, and that emasculated Yahoo Twist, prancing on his grave——"

Judith looked at her husband with interest—as she always did when his responses to a situation were what she called ethical and literary. "And the police too," she said. "Haven't they been busy putting slices of Limbert under a microscope?"

"Absolute rubbish. And now we'd better be——" Appleby broke off short. He had received the momentary—and altogether surprising—impression that a somewhat enlarged replica of the Buddha from the Da Vinci's window had been transformed into a self-guided missile and was about to make its kill in the pit of his stomach.

"John—this is Mr Brown, who has organised the exhibition."

The missile was now bobbing up and down with great rapidity, as if finally thrown off its course by an ingenious electronic device beneath Appleby's waistcoat. The proprietor of the Da Vinci was making a series of bows. Their elaboration suggested powerfully to Appleby that here was a world in which Judith was coming decidedly to count. Perhaps it had been her

11

name that the young reporter had been noting down, and not his at all.

"How do you do—yes?" Mr Braunkopf, who was bland, spherical and boneless, contrived to put such genuine solicitude into this conventional inquiry that it might well have been taken as referring to Appleby's bank-balance. "Lady Appleby is here our very goot freunt. Her advises are always goot advises—no?" Mr Braunkopf's eye darted swiftly round his gallery, as if to make quite sure that no even better and sager friend had a preferential claim on his attention. "And this is a most puttikler voonderble day—a birthday, Sir John and Lady Abbleby—yes?"

"A birthday?" Appleby, who had been working out that Mr Braunkopf must have enjoyed his nativity in the recesses of the continent and come thence to England by way of New York, was a little at sea with this reference, and disposed to wonder if he should say something about happy returns.

"A leg-end." Mr Braunkopf lowered his voice and tapped the topmost of the pile of catalogues he was carrying. "The birth of a leg-end, Sir John. Natchly I done few several big art deals my lonk career. But not never before the birth of a leg-end. The Limbert leg-end—that sounds goot, no? And now I have liddle time show you round. No—no inconveniences!" And Mr Braunkopf raised a soft white hand as if to discount the protestations of his gratified clients. "No inconveniences in the worlt. All these very important patrons and art people." The hand gestured in a manner that decidedly patronised the patrons indicated. "No doubt you much recognise other nobles gentry your goot freunts. The rests is from the continent. Collectors, *Kunsthistoriker*, directors some the biggest galleries, aircrafts of them come over due this great new leg-end." Mr Braunkopf's face lit up. It was plain that he was a man of imagination as well as commerce. He produced a gold watch. "Only now I wait Sir Kenneth, Sir Gerald, Dr Rothenstein. Till then I take you round."

This particular wait, Appleby suspected, would be a substantial one. But Judith appeared to like Mr Braunkopf, and he was not himself certain that he was prepared to disapprove of him. They therefore began a circuit of the room. It was still extremely crowded. In places like the Da Vinci the private views are by far the most public occasions of the year, and this particular private view held the additional attraction of being implicated with circumstances of some notoriety. Perhaps there would really grow up just such a Limbert legend as the resourceful Braunkopf was striving to create. To-day was certainly a good start. Braunkopf had mounted his exhibition with triumphant, if mildly indecent, speed. Gavin Limbert's funeral baked meats, had there been any, might well have furnished forth the discreet little buffet to which particularly favoured patrons might doubtless repair in an inner room.

Judith was looking at each picture with grave attention. A moment before, she had been much enjoying Mr Braunkopf; now she was entirely unaware of him. He appeared to be far from resenting this. Presumably he knew Judith as a person who sometimes bought pictures, but to whom pictures were never sold. Judith's husband, on the other hand, was an unknown quantity in this regard, and Mr Braunkopf felt that with him he was breaking new ground. Appleby, on his part, suspected that he would make

13

little of Gavin Limbert's technique, but might obtain quite a lot of instruction from Braunkopf's. Artistic fashions change, and for what was displayed on the walls around him Appleby was too old by a full generation. But human nature remains constant, and successful sales-talk must exploit the identical weaknesses to-day that the Serpent first hit upon in the Garden. Appleby knew that he must be offered the very same apple that diverted Eve. Braunkopf could do no more than serve it up with some garnish of his own.

"It is not so goot." The proprietor of the Da Vinci had paused before a picture on a corner of which—whether veraciously or not—one of his assistants had just affixed a small red star. "It has the genius, yes. It has the promises, yes." Mr Braunkopf looked hastily round about him, as if fearful that his next remark might be overheard by that one of his patrons whose faulty taste had prompted him to choose this particular Limbert for purchase. "But the performances, no."

"Doesn't really quite come off," Appleby said.

Mr Braunkopf replied only with a meaningful glance, such as passes in public between two persons tacitly cognizant that between them there has been forged a bond of superior understanding. Then he moved on, tapping his catalogue as he did so. "Limbert was yunk," he murmured discreetly. "Limbert was very yunk. And was he Raphael Sanzio, Sir John?" Mr Braunkopf made a full pause upon this question, as if to give Appleby time to come to a mature decision upon the point. "No—Limbert was not Raphael Sanzio."

"Not really dazzlingly precocious," Appleby hazarded. "Except, perhaps, now and then."

Mr Braunkopf's eyelids flickered. The effect was of

14

a man betraying despite himself some surprise at a suddenly revealed extreme perceptiveness in another. He paced on past a couple of pictures without inviting any attention to them. Then he paused before a third. With a stubby finger he pointed at one patch of it—an ellipse of pure vermilion. The finger moved across the canvas and paused on a cylindrical form in ultramarine, and from this it passed to an oblong in chrome yellow.

"Colour," Appleby offered.

The flicker presented itself more violently than before. And again Mr Braunkopf looked cautiously about him. "Colour," he said softly. "You are right, Sir John. It was when he gave himself to colour. In these first enthusiasticals"—and he gestured warily at the crowd now rather languidly circling the gallery—"there is not yet recognitions of it. But it is the truth. In colour there is Titian, and there is Gavin Limbert." For a moment Mr Braunkopf sank into what seemed a reverent aesthetic trance. And then he roused himself for an afterthought—the afterthought of a careful and fair-minded man. "And also there is Renoir—Renoir and our goot Mr Matthew Smith."

"And Giorgione?" Appleby was diffident.

"Ah—Giorgione." Mr Braunkopf frowned thoughtfully, as if here was a new idea, heterodox but perhaps significant—and certainly worthy of the most serious consideration in virtue of the high authority who had thought fit to propound it. Then his concentration relaxed, and his face lit up in recognition of a new intellectual truth. "But yes! It is goot, that, Sir John. It is very goot. Giorgione—he too was a colourist."

Judith had moved away. Perhaps Braunkopf was one of her established protégés of the moment, and

15

she disapproved of making fun of him. But they caught up with her before the large painting which had provided a background for the esoteric eloquence of Mervyn Twist. Twist was still there. Probably he was waiting for a cheque. Possibly he hoped for no more than a drink. Meanwhile he was favouring Judith with a species of technical appendix to his late address. "A definite advance, Lady Appleby. A big step forward. A substantial break with everything that he had been doing hitherto." Twist paused, evidently dissatisfied with the deplorable lucidity of these remarks. "A determined effort to disintegrate reality in the interest of the syncretic principle."

"Limbert's last picture." Braunkopf nudged Appleby in the ribs and whispered this information. "And his *chef-d'œuvre*. What pities, Sir John, if it shall go to America. Few several puttikler important persons want it for the Tate."

"Soaring," said Twist. "One sees the influence of the new transcendentalism, of Paul Klee, of the baroque interior, of aerial photography, of the schizophrenic dream."

"But the American galleries are hot on the stink." The guardian of the Limbert treasures managed to import much patriotic fervour into this confidence. At the same time he took a covert glance at Appleby's umbrella—always a good index of a man's financial standing. "An undisclosed sum," he murmured. "Some big public-spirituous person could buy this *chef-d'œuvre* by Limbert for an undisclosed sum to present it to the Tate. It would be in *The Times*, Sir John. Meritorious services to the worlt of art. Everyone would be pleased—and puttikler the kink and the queen."

16

Appleby, although one eminently well-affected towards the Throne, was not particularly drawn to this proposal. Perhaps this picture was really worthy to go to the Tate. He just wouldn't know. But he saw that it did represent some sort of departure from Limbert's usual manner; it was more crowded with intricate forms, and at the same time painted in a freer technique, than the others. When a wholly new idea came to an artist and excited him perhaps this was the sort of thing that happened. He glanced back at the pictures he had already seen, with the object of confirming his impression that in this last one Gavin Limbert had indeed been at something new. This action Mr Braunkopf chose to interpret after his own fashion. He took Appleby's arm with a sudden urgency which it was momentarily impossible to resist. "We go back," he said. "We go back that puttikler rich feast of colour you picked out for yourself, Sir John. Suppose you donate it as birthday-present to the Da Vinci's goot freunt Lady Abbleby, then the Da Vinci show its gratitude to two goot freunts by meeting you at a most surprising low figure."

They were now back before the picture that had prompted Mr Braunkopf to institute his comparison between the late Gavin Limbert and Titian. Appleby looked at it doubtfully. "What's it called?" he demanded.

Mr Braunkopf's eye lit up, and his clutch tightened on Appleby's arm. This, it seemed, was a stage in the selling of his wares that he was well-accustomed to and knew to be propitious. "Seagulls and Fish," he said confidently. "This rich meal of colour is called Seagulls and Fish. An oil on burlap."

"Burlap—what's that?" Appleby now sounded positively suspicious.

"Very hard wearing." Mr Braunkopf met him instantly on his own ground. "All this wonderful rich indigestible banquet of colour last you a long time. One hundred guineas. And Lady Abbleby would think you gave two, three hundred."

"I see." Appleby, who had been feeling with some compunction that he ought not for his own entertainment to detain Braunkopf from more likely prey, a little hardened at this suggestion. "And the big one—what's that called?"

"The *chef-d'œuvre*?" Braunkopf's eye kindled further. At the same time he hedged, having evidently neglected the crucial matter of nomenclature in this particular instance. "It is an abstraction, Sir John—an abstraction in a voonderble new artistic manner."

"I think a picture should have a name." Appleby appeared to lose interest.

"But certainly it has a name." And Braunkopf smiled reassuringly, while his eye simultaneously sought inspiration from the ceiling. "The Fifth Day of Creation. This puttikler voonderble last great picture by Limbert is called that. The Sixth Day of Creation."

"I thought you said the Fifth."

"Both." Braunkopf was firm. "The Fifth and Sixth Days of Creation. This voonderble picture is an abstraction. And time is an abstraction too."

"But not the price?"

"I beg your pardons?" Braunkopf looked at Appleby with what was perhaps a first gleam of suspicion.

"What would it cost—to buy and give to the Tate?"

Braunkopf took a deep breath. He had the air of a man whose faith in the ultimate goodness of human nature, heroically preserved through much disillusion, was about to be justified. "We go back," he said. "This all very fine." He waved a dismissive hand at Seagulls and Fish. "But nothing but colour, Sir John. No form. And form is the soul of art. We go back to look at this great *chef-d'œuvre* where Limbert at last masters form."

"I don't think we do."

They had taken a couple of paces across the gallery. Braunkopf was startled. "What you say, Sir John?"

"I don't think we do go back to it. It's not there."

This was true. There was still a considerable crowd in the room, but a momentary parting in it allowed them a clear view of the opposite wall. The palette, wreath, and big black bow were still in evidence. But the space beneath them was empty.

Braunkopf gave a howl of rage and darted across the room. Judith, who had just shaken off Mervyn Twist, rejoined her husband. "John—whatever have you done to Braunkopf? Driven him mad?"

"The Fifth and Sixth Days of the Creation has vanished. And it disturbs him. I had just asked the price. It must be mortifying to have a large painting evaporate when you think you've had a nibble after it. But here he comes again."

"Gone—stolen!" A doting parent, who returns home to find his only child absconded with a ruffian, could not have put more pathos into these words than did Mr Hildebert Braunkopf or Brown. "Sir John, Lady Abbleby, this *chef-d'œuvre* of Limbert has been departed with by thieves!"

"Are you quite sure?" Appleby did not seem disposed to any very marked professional curiosity. "Per-

19

haps the people at the Tate were so impatient that they just sent along for it?"

"You make a joking, Sir John." Braunkopf was deeply reproachful.

"And you, Mr Brown, perhaps make a sensation? Limbert is really having a wonderful time. First he gets killed, and then his chief picture disappears at this private view. Get busy with the reporters, my dear sir, in time for the final extra."

"It is publicities, yes—this great disaster to art?" Whether ingenuously or not, Braunkopf appeared to be catching at a suddenly perceived crumb of comfort.

"It certainly is." Appleby's voice had gone a shade grim. "You might suggest to the newspaper people that they headline it as the mystery of the abstracted abstraction. . . . Judith, we'll be getting along."

2

Some three hours later Appleby initialled the last of a pile of reports, picked up a pipe, filled it, and thrust the tobacco-jar across his broad desk to Detective-Inspector Cadover. "Anything turned up?" he asked. It was the formula ushering in the day's final, and unofficial, review of the work of the department.

"Some security people worried about the Waterbath Research Station. They say small boys have been getting in and taking photographs."

Appleby smiled. "If the government must publicise the making of those things it's not to be expected that small boys won't show a healthy curiosity."

"I pointed that out, and asked whether they were supposing the existence of a juvenile spy-ring. They said one of the boys had been caught, and had seemed to have a foreign accent. They said it was thought to be Polish. I asked if it might have been Welsh. They said it might have been. I suggested that they find out. They said they couldn't, because the boy had run away. A pretty confession."

Appleby struck a match. "It certainly seems a bit feeble."

"I asked how he had managed to run away. They hedged a bit. But I saw how it had happened. Lord Buffery himself had strayed in on their nonsense and connived at the boy's going peaceably home to his mother. But of course those people are as nervous as cats, and they think that the Director made an error of judgment. I said that it was their duty to tell him so. At that, they went away." Cadover gave a gloomy sigh. The fatuity of what he called security people was a constant occasion of real sorrow to him. He regarded it as one prominent expression of a general decay of intelligence characteristic of the age. Since the departure of the apocalyptically minded Hudspith from Scotland Yard this mantle had largely descended to him.

"Anything else?"

"The Duke of Horton called. He wanted to see you, and wouldn't talk to anybody else. I suggested the Commissioner, but he said he didn't like him. He must be very eccentric."

"Because he doesn't like the Commissioner?"

"I hadn't that in mind." Cadover stuffed his own pipe with a steady hand poised beneath a poker face. "The Duke left you a message to say that somebody had stolen his aquarium and goldfish and silverfish. He must be very eccentric to come up from Berkshire just to report a thing like that."

"It seems a bit odd."

"I ventured to say that I didn't know he was an ichthyologist. He gave me a queer look, and said that we seemed to keep some odd fish in the C.I.D. But his manner was extremely courteous."

"Was it indeed?" Appleby appeared interested. "That means he must be really perturbed. . . . Anything more?"

"Old Lady Clancarron."

"Oh, dear!"

"Yes. She said that her Council was increasingly concerned over the present immorality and profaneness of the English stage. I suggested she see the Lord Chamberlain. She said the Lord Chamberlain was little better than a reprobate, and in the pocket of the Archbishops, who are fanatical play-goers. So I advised trying the P.M. She's probably in Downing Street now. I don't think there's been anything else. Except something about a picture—the theft of a picture from some gallery or other this afternoon. It seems to have happened"—Cadover was at his most inexpressive—"in the presence of quite a distinguished gathering."

"And also of Judith and myself?"

Quite faintly, Cadover smiled. Then he fished from his pocket a folded evening paper. "Wonderful likenesses these fellows manage to get nowadays." He smoothed out the paper and handed it to his chief. "They actually got you while you were looking at the very picture that was going to be stolen a few minutes later. A stroke of luck, that."

Appleby studied his own likeness on the open front page before him. It might be a good likeness, but he felt that the expression had got somewhat out of hand. He had the appearance of contemplating The Fifth and Sixth Days of Creation with something between large admiration and holy awe. Judith was not in the photograph, nor Mervyn Twist. But Hildebert Braunkopf was well to the fore, in a pose judiciously compounded of massive mercantile probity and delicate artistic feeling. Appleby handed back the paper without visible emotion. "Stolen?" he said. "Isn't that jumping to a conclusion? This little Brown or Braunkopf is playing up the Limbert affair for all it is worth. It struck me that this was just his notion of keeping the pot boiling."

Cadover shook his head. "We sent a man along—and he reported to me before I came in. His guess is that the picture really has been stolen. . . . Look at the middle page."

Appleby took the paper again and looked. Another press photographer, it appeared, had enjoyed a profitable afternoon at the Da Vinci. This picture was of an elderly and respectable tradesman, dressed in a white apron, engaged in hoisting what was discernibly The Fifth and Sixth Days of Creation into a covered van. A small crowd of curious spectators watched him. And these were being somewhat officiously held back by a policeman.

"It was quite simple," Cadover said. "This fellow simply walked into the gallery, took the picture from the wall, and walked away with it. Nobody thought to question him. And the police, as you see, can be represented as having pretty well bowed him out. The papers will make quite a thing of it."

"I'm sure they will."

"In fact, it's already fairly brightly written up in this one." Cadover spoke with mournful satisfaction. "Listen. *It is understood that the authorities at Scotland Yard are somewhat baffled by the problem of issuing a description of the missing Limbert. It is a very mod-*

24

ern and highly abstract work of art, which may now be described as elusive in more senses than one. When traced, however, there should be no difficulty over identification, since the Yard's own Sir John Appleby, now an Assistant Commissioner of Police, happens to have been inspecting it closely only a few minutes before the theft (see picture). It is understood that Sir John was proposing to purchase the work for presentation to the National Gallery, Milbank.'" Cadover paused. "Now, that's a very interesting thing. Had the Tate agreed to take it?"

"I didn't ask. The business of my thinking of buying the picture is pure invention by this enterprising Braunkopf. Or rather"—Appleby was candid—"not *pure* invention, because I was playing the fool rather, while the chap was showing me round. In fact, it's a fair cop. And as I look like hearing a good deal about Gavin Limbert, perhaps you'd better tell me about him. You remember I haven't been into the case in any detail."

"There isn't much detail." Cadover set down his pipe and fixed his gaze upon the ceiling. He enjoyed exposition. "And if it wasn't for this girl who has disappeared—her name is Arrow, Mary Arrow—there would hardly be a case either. Limbert may very well have shot himself. Artists do that sort of thing from time to time."

"I doubt whether many do it more than once. Had Limbert?"

"Had he shown any disposition to take his own life before? Well, no—not that we've managed to hear of. But it's not much of a point."

Appleby nodded. "I agree. Only, in this Da Vinci place, they have a photograph of him that I happened

25

to take a good look at this afternoon. I judged it more informative than his paintings; and it suggested a lad whom the world wasn't treating at all hardly. Was there any occasion for suicide—disease, debts, trouble with a girl?"

"It doesn't appear that there was. I was thinking that he might have felt that he had come to the end of his inspiration—that sort of thing." Cadover advanced this hypothesis without much confidence. "But I've made inquiries; and I'm told that when a young painter feels like that he doesn't often do more than go out and get drunk."

"Had Limbert been out getting drunk?"

"There was no alcohol in the body. For that matter, there was none in his studio either. But it did look as if he'd had some sort of brain-storm. Everything all over the place."

"Artists are often untidy—much oftener untidy than suicidal."

"But Limbert was an exception there. I've checked up on it. People say that he was an orderly young man. He'd been two years in the navy, and they say he took back into civilian life the sort of habits you learn there. Everything having its place."

"Even a girl?"

"Even this girl Mary Arrow. No evidence that he was badly worked up about her. The man down below told me that Gavin—that's Limbert, you know—had liked her thighs. I felt a bit out of my depth"—Cadover was still staring at the ceiling—"so I gave the point particular attention. This man down below felt that it was what you might call a purely artistic liking. Were there any—um—undraped studies at the Da Vinci?"

"Were there any nudes? If there were, they had been decidedly disintegrated in the interest of the syncretic principle. That's the current phrase, by the way, for banishing anything recognisable from a painting. You'd better know."

"I'll make a note of it." Cadover was seriously interested. "Well, Limbert painted this girl—or anyway her thighs—and sometimes he took her out to a meal."

"She's a professional model?"

"No. She's by way of being a musician, and she lives—or until she disappeared she lived—right at the top. You ought to come and see the place."

"We'll go now. I'll get a car." Appleby picked up a telephone. "Carry on."

"I thought you'd be expected home to dinner." Beneath the faint irony of a bachelor Cadover masked considerable gratification at this alacrity. "I asked if it was usual for girls who weren't models to be painted in that way. This man—the man down below—said No, not very. But he supposed Miss Arrow to be a perfectly respectable person. She just dropped in on Limbert from time to time to lend a hand—or, as you might say, a thigh."

"It all sounds quite freezingly innocent. But Mary Arrow has nevertheless vanished?"

"Completely. She seems to have walked out of her flat with no more ado than if she had been going round the corner for half a pint of milk. There are relations beginning to make a fuss—and quite rightly. Of course this isn't so very long ago. Limbert has been dead just ten days. The girl may simply have lost her nerve and bolted somewhere for a while. She may have reckoned that she might have to appear at an

27

inquest and explain about acting as a model. And modesty——"

"Perhaps so. You mean she may have felt that it would distress her old father, the clergyman—that sort of thing?"

Cadover was surprised. "I hadn't gathered that you knew——"

"They are usually out of country rectories, girls like that. But presumably she would have reckoned that her old father would be even more upset when she just vanished." Appleby got up and moved over to his hat and coat. "I think it queer."

"But one can't call it much to go on. The probability is that Limbert *did* shoot himself. He was shot through the roof of the mouth, almost at point-blank range, and the revolver was lying on the floor beside him."

"Navy type?"

"No. And nothing else to connect him with it either."

"Finger-prints?"

"You may remember one doesn't often get anything one can call a print on those things with heavily cross-hatched bone butts." Cadover spoke as to one who had long passed lamentably above and beyond the practical investigation of crime. "And there weren't any unexplained finger-prints anywhere in the studio either."

"In fact your guess is suicide in a fit of depression?"

"It's certainly what the coroner will put into the heads of his jury at the adjourned inquest." Cadover was cautious. "I wouldn't say more than that it's the superficial picture, however. There may be something quite different beneath the surface."

A low purr came from an instrument on Appleby's

desk. "There's the car," he said. "Limbert's place was in Chelsea? We can be there in ten minutes—and give the Tate a wave on the way."

Gas Street is a cul-de-sac running parallel to King's Road, and is approached from a quiet street which itself comes to a dead end before reaching the river. Despite the utilitarian associations of its name, it is far from being deficient in a sense of style. One side, indeed, is frankly a line of mews, and at the bottom is nothing more striking than a high, blank brick wall pierced by a single small and unobtrusive door. The remaining aspect, however, is attractive—and attractive after a fashion characteristic of the district. It is a terrace of diminutive, high, narrow houses, with frontages which are neither drearily identical nor planned in disregard each of the other, for they belong to a period of admirable taste in the unobtrusive domestic facade. Moreover Gas Street is inhabited by people decidedly proud of their proprietorship of these mild architectural amenities. In the whole street there are no two front doors painted in the same hue. But—correspondingly— there is no jarring note from end to end—the colours blending or contrasting with each other and with the mellow brick or clean stucco around them in an exhibition of the nicest taste. In Gas Street, in fact, a good deal of fuss is made over that sort of thing. Areas that are in themselves no more than narrow and gloomy pits are turned ingeniously into miniature shrubberies, and up the railings that guard them interesting creepers ramify from gaily painted tubs. Frequently small objects of statuary, valuable whether from their antiquity or their intrinsic merit, are boldly exposed upon the very fringe of the foot-path, just as if they were of no more account than the gnomes and frogs and rabbits, similarly obtruded by other classes of society. And it is plain to the most casual passer-by that the Gas Street interiors must exhibit an answering refinement. Most of the lower windows are seldom curtained, and one may peer—perhaps over a line of diminutive cacti, or of delicate fantasies in finely blown glass—into tiny rooms where every object is the fruit of vigilant artistic consideration. Provincial persons, seeking to gratify their young with a view of the red-coated pensioners of Chelsea Hospital, and taking the single wrong turning that lands them in this impressive blind alley, are frequently so overawed by its per-vasive refinement that they may be observed re-treating from it on tiptoe.

There must be much quiet prosperity tucked away in Gas Street. On a Friday evening it is lined with cars of all but the most expensive sort, and into these the inhabitants may be seen packing themselves and quite surprising numbers of children in preparation for departure to some week-end cottage adapted to the same species of comfortably Lilliputian house-keeping. It was this spectacle—that of the sardine era in the history of the English upper middle class—that greeted Appleby and Cadover as they approached their destination.

"It doesn't look at all like what they call the scene of the crime." Appleby peered out at a chromium-plated baby-carriage being hoisted to the roof of a large black saloon. "Too overpoweringly respectable altogether. I don't feel that policemen have any busi-ness here."

Cadover chuckled. "There's a funny thing now," he said. "As it happens, Gas Street was stuffing with police on the very night that Limbert died."

"Stuffing with police?"

"Yes. The fact is going to emerge a trifle uncomfortably if the coroner really spreads himself. A policeman, you might say, at the bottom of every area, and another perched up on every lamp-post."

"Why on earth——"

"Lady Clancarron."

"Bless my soul!"

"You see that brick wall at the end of the road? There's a night-club through there—the Thomas Carlyle."

"I think I've heard of it. But it seems a queer name for a night-club."

"No doubt it's felt to be rather a smart joke." Cadover made this sage observation bear the air of a sombre rebuke of the frivolous classes. "Of course there's nothing Turnell and his people don't know about it. But Lady Clancarron got it into her head that the place is a haunt of the most extreme vice. And she worried the Home Secretary until he begged the Commissioner to lay on a really big show. So that night the place was sealed off as if it contained Guy Fawkes and a whole Gunpowder Plot. And Lady Clancarron and poor Turnell directed the raid between them from a radio-equipped car on the Embankment. It was while the whole police force of the division, more or less, was poking into dust-bins in search of half a bottle of whisky that this chap Limbert was coming to his mysterious end. If you hadn't been off hobnobbing with foreigners you'd have heard about it."

"I've noticed the Commissioner being mum about something." Appleby reached for the door handle. "And Limbert had his studio in one of these natty dwellings? Not quite the sort of Chelsea I'd imagined for him."

"It rather breaks down at these last two houses." Cadover climbed out of the car after Appleby. "Limbert's flat is in the one at the end—one floor up. The house hasn't been modernised or improved at all, and the rents are quite low. Counting Limbert and Mary Arrow, there were four tenants in the place. And all artistic."

Appleby shook his head. "Surely not. It's the dressy people up the road who are artistic. Limbert and his friends I take to have been artists."

"Wouldn't it be the business of artists to be artistic?" Cadover looked at his chief with all the appearance of serious inquiry.

"They leave that to the mugs. Do we go straight in?"

"Straight in, sir, and up to the first floor." Without ceremony, Cadover threw open the front door of the last house in Gas Street. "What they call bijou."

To Appleby the gem-like quality of the place was scarcely apparent. But it was certainly on a small scale. There was a door on the left, a door straight in front, and a narrow staircase edging its way up the wall on the right. On this wall the presence of creative activity at once declared itself, since somebody had enriched it with a rapidly executed Crucifixion in modern dress. Cadover eyed this with disfavour—as well he might, for the Roman soldiery were represented by a variety of criminal types in the uniform of the metropolitan police. "You might gaol the chap who did that," he said. "It's uttering an obscene advertisement. Six months."

Appleby shook his head. "I doubt it. We're in a private house."

"It's what you might call a common staircase." Cadover was obstinate. "Six months, or even——"

"*Dead* common."

They turned. The door on the left had opened, and displayed an unshaven man in a blue blouse. Cadover looked at him with a sort of modified rancour. "Good evening, Mr Boxer. The Assistant Commissioner is in charge of this affair now."

Mr Boxer, rightly interpreting this as a form of introduction, nodded affably to Appleby and then turned again to Cadover. "Lot of jaw," he said.

Cadover frowned. "I'm aware that a good many questions have had to be asked——"

"No, no. Your friend the commissionaire. Lot of jaw, and that long upper lip. Velasquez—in modern dress too."

"*Commissioner*." Cadover was incensed. "From Scotland Yard."

"You don't say so?" The unshaven man showed interest. "They keep one at the door of the Thomas Carlyle. But I didn't think you'd have them at the Yard—just use bobbies. Won't you come in?" And Mr Boxer stepped aside with the most perfect friendliness. "I'm a bit stuck, to tell you the truth. And Grace is beginning to sulk. You may clear the air."

At this Appleby took the initiative. "Yes," he said, "I think we'll come in. Got a good light?"

"Damned awful—see for yourself." They had entered a room of something less than moderate size, appropriated to the uses of a painter's studio. "I have

33

to break it in through all that gauze. And that's why the values keep going wrong, if you ask me. Just take a look at them." And Boxer pointed in gloomy distaste at a large canvas standing on an easel. "Pitiful."

Appleby took a look. The picture-space was entirely occupied by what appeared to be the representation of a work of statuary in an improbable green marble. The figure, a female one, was ingeniously contorted so as to provide the form of a solid cube; and the effect was the more striking in that the subject seemed to be an advanced case of dropsy complicated by elephantiasis. The upper limbs had approximately the same girth as the torso, and the neck had a greater circumference than the head. Appleby cast round for an appropriate word. "Chunky," he said.

"Of course that was the *idea*." Boxer shook his head sombrely. "I got it from one of those tinplate advertisements in a railway-station, showing a pound of pre-war sausages done up square. It made me think of Grace at once. By the way, *that's* Grace. Miss Brooks to you."

Appleby glanced across the studio. Reclined on a divan was a young woman of proportions surprisingly like those disposed on Boxer's canvas. One felt at once that she ought to be reminiscent of a fat lady in a circus—and in the same instant one realised that this was an entirely inappropriate comparison. Miss Brooks was chunky—preternaturally chunky—and not fat; in fact she was the very fleshly embodiment of ideas that had begun to spread themselves over canvas and insinuate themselves into stone somewhere in the early 1920s. It was, Appleby reflected, what always happened. Rossetti stunners had begun getting themselves born just about the time when

Dante Gabriel himself was giving over. . . . But this train of reflection must not be allowed to induce an impolite silence. "Good evening," Appleby said.

Miss Brooks blinked. She appeared to be in a sort of stupor or coma. Or perhaps it was a rigor. In deference to the arrival of non-professional visitors she had drawn some species of light wrapping round her monumental limbs: nevertheless these were discernibly still disposed in approximately the attitude displayed on the canvas. Miss Brooks blinked again. "Evening," she said dully—and turning her eyes but not her head towards Boxer added, "Is it the rent?"

"Not the rent—the police." Speaking absently, Boxer walked over to Miss Brooks and peered glumly between her shoulder-blades. "If you could just flex a thought more *there*——"

"I've flexed till I'm never likely to unflex again." That Miss Brooks was indeed disposed to sulk now became apparent. "I told you at the grocer's it was no good. I told you the moment we saw the thing."

"It's that confounded crate." Boxer, turning back to Appleby, pointed to a small cage-like structure in the middle of the floor. "I had to give three bob for it—the only perfect cube in the shop. But Grace won't go in—or not without getting rolls of flesh where they're no good to me. I've shoved and I've pummelled, but she just won't go. It's the shoulders. She *bulges*—just where I want to get the articulation of the humerus and the scapula like M. A. Buonarroto himself."

"That must be one of the Glasgow crowd living off the Euston Road." Miss Brooks, although still dazed, appeared to consider it only civil to give this explanation to the laity. "Boxer's always mad about them."

35

"What about putting her in head-first?" Boxer's gloomy features suddenly displayed genuine artistic inspiration. "We could get more purchase, shoving hard on her behind. Particularly with three of us on the job. Get up, Grace. I believe we've got it."

Miss Brooks—although with obvious reluctance—prepared herself to comply. Cadover looked at Appleby in alarm. "Perhaps, sir——"

"Quite so." Appleby, although perfectly ready to assist an artist in the pursuit of his plastic idea, felt that it was hardly fair not to come to his subordinate's relief. "We'll get along upstairs. But if Miss Brooks doesn't mind resting for another couple of minutes, perhaps we might have a word or two with Mr Boxer about this fellow Limbert."

"Must you people really go on chewing over Gavin?" Somewhat unexpectedly, Boxer produced a packet of cigarettes and hospitably dispensed them to the company. "He's been terribly lucky."

"Lucky?" Cadover was perplexed.

"He's dead, isn't he?"

The simplicity of this left Cadover momentarily without a reply, and Appleby interposed. "You take rather a poor view of the human situation, Mr Boxer?"

"I don't know anything about situations—except the one I started off in. That was in a draper's shop, and it was bloody awful. But if you mean *life*, you're barking up the wrong tree. Life's all right. You should get into training for a bit, and then try it."

Just as real life labours after art, Appleby reflected, so do artists labour after literature. At least young artists do. In each generation they find their Portrait of an Artist in the work of some accomplished novelist—and then they live up to it hard. Boxer was doing that, and it would be naive to be offended by him. "But about Limbert?" he asked mildly.

"He'd set his heart on being a painter. That's why he's lucky to be dead. Not on painting—but on being a painter, with books written about him for the edification of posterity. Pitiful." Boxer reflected. "Not that he wasn't a genius in his way."

"A genius?" Cadover interrupted with involuntary respect. "Limbert's painting was really good?"

"Pitiful. A nice Cambridge boy, who had made squiggles in his notebooks between lectures on Julius Caesar and more lectures on Caesar Augustus. And held an exhibition above a tea-shop. And was told by all the wives of all the professors that he was a True Artist. So he went to Paris, and worked ever so hard at the squiggles and wriggles and squirts—determined, you might say, to teach the worms their business. Now they're teaching Gavin. Only he *did* have a genius. For being a nice Cambridge boy."

Appleby received this picturesque speech thoughtfully. "Do you mean that he was dead set on doing really well as a painter—so dead set that disillusion would have been very bitter to him?"

"I say he was dead set on *being* a painter—and a great one. So when he cracked up on that he wouldn't have had the consolation of just *painting*. He's well out of it."

"You mean that——"

"Oh, to hell with what I mean! Gavin's dead, isn't he? Let be, man." Boxer strode across the studio and gave the grocer's crate a vicious kick. "I think I'll have to put Grace into a double cube, after all. Disgustingly dull work. But if she won't fit, she won't. Impossible to shave her down, unfortunately. If you prick her, she bleeds."

"Limbert bled. Through the ceiling." Miss Brooks had sunk back again upon the divan, but this time without much troubling to veil her marmoreal splendours. "Zhitkov was furious."

"Zhitkov?" Appleby looked at Cadover.

"A sculptor who lives across the passage. Limbert's studio was just above him."

"And Limbert dripped on his Venus." It was Miss Brooks who continued in this informative vein. "Zhitkov was really mad at him for being so inconsiderate. He says that blood is the one thing you can't get out of a stone."

"Gavin had a right to drip where he chose." Boxer spoke with mournful indignation. "And, anyway, Zhitkov's carvings are utterly——" Words seemed to fail him.

"Pitiful?" Cadover offered this with large irony.

Boxer looked surprised. "Exactly," he said. "You've hit on a damned good way of putting it. Pitiful. He ought to stick to his waxworks. But I'd nearly forgotten. Grace has something to say. In fact she has been wanting to make a statement to the police. I've told her not to be silly."

Cadover frowned. "That was most improper."

"Rubbish. The only statement that Grace is qualified to make is a purely spacial one. In a cube. But, as you're here, perhaps she'd better talk. It may sweeten her up a bit. Grace—state away."

Thus abjured, Miss Brooks sat up and folded her wrap around her. "There was a man stalking Limbert," she said. "All that day. He was coming down the stairs as I came in to sit for Boxer about ten. It

38

sounded as if Limbert was turning him out. 'You can't say it isn't a fair offer,' he was saying. 'It sounds to me much more like a foul one,' Limbert said. 'I don't understand you,' he said. 'Oh, don't you?' Limbert said. 'You're taking unnecessary offence,' he said. 'If you think I can't take a guess at what this is about,' Limbert said, 'you must think I'm a fool.' 'I'll double it,' he said—and it seemed to me he sounded pretty desperate. 'Double it?' Limbert said; 'double it? You can double, double, toil and trouble it out of this.' 'It wasn't a valid purchase,' he said, 'and I can bring in the law.' 'You can go and eat yourself,' Limbert said. Or at least he said something like that. And then he pushed the chap out of the front door there."

"One moment." Cadover raised in an admonitory way the pencil with which he had been taking short-hand notes. "This will be transcribed and read back to you and you'll be asked to sign it—see?"

"I should hope so. And I'll expect it to be in the papers too." Miss Brooks was indignant. "For that's not all. The chap stayed skulking about in one or other of those mews opposite, pretty well all day."

"We ought to have been told about this long ago. Can you describe the man's appearance?"

"He was middle-aged and ordinary looking and in the usual sort of clothes."

"What do you mean by the usual sort of clothes?"

"Just ordinary ones. I think he had a grey overcoat. And there was nothing special about him. If he'd had a bad limp, or a glass eye, or a horrible scar across one cheek I'm sure I'd have noticed it."

"No doubt. By the way, Miss Brooks, at what hour did you leave Gas Street yourself that day?"

"I was back here for Boxer in the afternoon. I

stopped to do him a fry about eight—you'd think any man could do himself a fry, but he can't—so that it was dark by the time I left. That chap might have been lurking about the place still."

"Thank you." Cadover closed his notebook with an impressive snap. "The Assistant Commissioner and I are now going upstairs. But we may want another word with both of you in half-an-hour's time."

Boxer, who had returned to stare darkly at his canvas, looked up at this. "That's all right," he said. "Any time. We shan't insist on the presence of our solicitor." And he accompanied his visitors politely to the door. In the passage his eye fell on the Crucifixion opposite. "Mind you," he broke out suddenly, "there was nothing wrong with Gavin's painting. No vice in it. A daub like *that* gave him a pain in the neck. But—well, paint hadn't been given him in his cradle. That's all."

Cadover had turned to the staircase. Suddenly he stopped. "Mr Boxer, there is one further thing I must ask you now. Did Miss Brooks in fact leave your studio at eight o'clock, or did she stay—later?"

Boxer stared. Then he broke into a laugh. "I see," he said. "I quite see. *La vie de Boheme*, as pictured in the Police Gazette. I assure you that Grace is utterly virtuous. The perfect cube, warranted free from distracting erotic associations. You have only to look at her, after all. Brooks too broad for leaping, as the poet says. So long."

Cadover made no reply, but stumped up the stairs behind Appleby. Even more than commonly, there was a heavy deliberation in his tread.

3

Here a man had died, mysteriously. Probably he had been murdered—standing on this floor. Appleby found that he had almost forgotten the sensation of entering such a room. And quite suddenly Gavin Limbert, whom he had never seen nor would ever see, became real to him. The people downstairs, the crush at the Da Vinci, Cadover glowering beside him, even Judith at home bathing the children: these had all become for the time background figures, lightly washed in behind the solid form of the unknown dead man. Limbert, pale and resolved, thrusting a revolver against his palate. Limbert, his eyebrows raised in astonishment, opening his mouth to speak, to cry out. . . . There were these and other hypothetical pictures. Only one could correspond with the actual fact of the matter. But for the moment they were all grimly real—as real as the spinning plug of lead that had instantaneously ripped apart mind and matter in a young man's brain.

Limbert had occupied the whole of this floor. It was in fact no more than one long room, running north and south and with windows at each end, but with an archway and curtains indicating an indecisive division into a studio and a bedroom. Opening off the studio end was a tiny kitchen, and off the bedroom end an equally tiny bathroom: these occupied, actually, no more than the breadth of the staircase outside. Appleby saw at once that it was a desirable place. The length was useful, and the north window had been properly enlarged and raised to the ceiling. Limbert had no doubt been living on threepence—the evidences of orthodox artistic indigence were not lacking—but he had not been living on twopence, as Boxer down below had no doubt long been constrained to do. The studio was entirely masculine in suggestion, with a minimum of furniture, functionally arranged and chosen on severely utilitarian principles. But there was nothing austere about it, or aloof; one could readily people it, in imagination, with the dead man's Cambridge friends, ironical but secretly impressed before the spectacle of the new world in which Gavin had established himself; or with hovering aunts, presenting themselves only upon due notice, bearing pots of jam or—upon high occasions—bottles of decayed wine abstracted from some deceased uncle's cellar. Limbert's own work had all disappeared, swept away by the astute Braunkopf. But there was a scattering of pictures on the walls, disposed in the random manner favoured by painters; these were mostly reproductions of drawings, pen and ink over silverpoint, by Leonardo. Over the fireplace was a small oilpainting of a gentleman in a curricle, with a groom holding the horses' heads. Appleby walked over and examined this. "No," he said. "The lad can't have been in any anxiety about to-morrow's breakfast. Perhaps he only had this on loan from his family. But, if so, they trusted him with it, and must have been on good terms with him. It's a Stubbs."

"Valuable?" Cadover eyed the picture with provisional respect.

"Decidedly. Stubbs is all the go. So it's significant that this stayed put."

"We thought of robbery. You see, sir, either Limbert had suffered a bit of a brain-storm or the place had been ransacked by the person who attacked him. Everything was at sixes and sevens. If you look at the books that have been put back on the shelves there, you'll see they've been pitched all over the place, and half the spines broken."

Appleby looked at the books. They were a mixed lot: school prizes, mostly for woodwork or mathematics; a German history of art in a dozen battered volumes; three or four expensive monographs on modern abstract painters; a complete Conrad; a dozen books of verse, preponderantly by Auden and Day Lewis; a litter of Penguins; a shelf of miscellaneous French books, mostly in paper covers. Appleby made a systematic examination. "Do you think," he asked presently, "that Limbert would get so excited when reading an improper book that he would rip open the pages with his fingers?"

Cadover considered a suitable reply to this. "I can't judge. But I hope not."

"Ever read Sade's *Justine, ou les Malheurs de la Vertu?*"

"Certainly not."

"Here it is, with about a hundred pages carefully

43

cut and the rest torn open anyhow. What do you make of that?"

"Limbert read a hundred pages and got bored. Then somebody else attacked the thing not as a reader but as a searcher."

Appleby nodded. "Precisely. And there are several other books that have been served in the same way. There *was* a search—and for something so small that it could have been slipped up between the uncut pages of a book."

Cadover scratched his jaw. "Or at least so slender that it could have been torn up and distributed in that way. Things like these, for instance." He pointed to the Leonardo drawings pinned to the wall. "Or a diary, or letters, or a will."

"Or a good many other things. Let's take it as established that the studio was combed for some small object or a set of small objects. It makes the theory of a brain-storm followed by suicide unlikely, although not impossible." Appleby frowned at the book still in his hand. "He read a hundred pages of *Justine* and then gave over. Probably had a go at Conrad instead. And that yarn about his showing some shifty character the door. It sounded all right, don't you think? In fact a nice lad with honourable if injudicious ambitions, just as that fellow Boxer describes him. Why should he suddenly have his brains scattered by a revolver bullet?" Appleby strode to the big north window and stared out. The last light was fading from a low London sky, and the rumble of traffic from King's Road was like that of some clumsy stage machinery letting down a curtain of darkness over Chelsea. "Let me have the picture, Cadover, as it came to us."

44

"It starts with this fellow Zhitkov, who has the room down below, next to Boxer."

"Zhitkov is beneath one part of this and Boxer beneath the other?"

"Quite correct, sir. Well, at about nine o'clock on the morning of Tuesday the 23rd of October—ten days ago, that is—Zhitkov presented himself at the local station, looking like a ghost. He said there was blood pouring through his ceiling. That was a new one on the station sergeant, who answered, very truly, that blood just doesn't behave in that way. But Zhitkov was thoroughly shaken, and a constable came back with him to see what it was all about. Sure enough, on Zhitkov's ceiling, which was in uncommonly poor repair, there was a small brown stain. And from it something really had dripped on a piece of statuary below. It was no more than a drop or two, but the constable had a kind of feeling that it *was* blood, human or other. So up he came to investigate. Limbert's door was locked—a Yale lock—and there was no reply to any amount of knocking. The constable was just going away to report when Boxer appeared with a spare key. He kept one hanging in his studio, it seemed, so that he could show Limbert's stuff to any possible clients or dealers when Limbert was out. A friendly—and as you might say optimistic—arrangement."

Appleby nodded. "Certainly optimistic. But quite a common arrangement among studio folk."

"Well, Boxer opened the door and walked in, with the constable and Zhitkov following. Limbert was lying dead on the floor, just where you're standing now, sir. There was a good deal of congealed blood—and some of it had actually got through a crack in the boards and advertised itself down below. The doctors decided that Limbert had been shot early in the small hours—perhaps round about two o'clock. And the whole place was turned upside down, as I've said. It certainly looked like murder. And a murderer—or a whole band of them—could have got away·easily enough. They had only to walk out, closing the door behind them, and troop downstairs."

"What about the street door?"

"Nobody bothers about it, and it stays unlocked all night. There was another route they could have taken as well—but didn't. Have a look at that south window, sir."

Appleby turned away from the large north window and crossed the room. A light iron fire-escape ran down from the upper storeys and past the south window to a deserted yard below. "I see. Not very usual in these small houses."

"At some time in the past the whole building was used as a little sweat-shop. Dozens of wretched girls cooped up in the attics sewing, so that an escape was required by regulations. As you see, this window has stout old-fashioned wooden shutters on the inside. Limbert quite often had them closed, because he didn't want light from that way. And they've got heavy bolts—put on for security, I suppose, when the fire-escape was erected. When the body was found, the shutters were closed and the window bolted. So nobody did actually make off that way. And that's the whole story, so far as the purely local investigation is concerned."

"Not much of a story."

"I agree." Cadover nodded gloomily. "But there's the fact that we have to accept. Until this girl Grace

46

Brooks told us that yarn a few minutes ago there was just nobody round about here prepared to witness to anything unusual. Except, of course, the police raid on the Thomas Carlyle."

"Ah."

"Everybody who was still awake at midnight knew that there was something on *there*, and perhaps that made them indisposed to notice anything else."

"Unfortunate."

"It just shows that the Commissioner should steer clear of crackpot ideas put up to him by influential ladies of title." Cadover was unusually tart.

"That's one way of looking at it. But might this raid have had any other influence on the affair?" Appleby, who was now prowling restlessly round the studio, stopped and looked enquiringly at Cadover. "Have you considered that?"

"Thoroughly, I hope. And it is just possible that somebody knowing about the raid in advance—and who mightn't, with Lady Clancarron on the job?—saw it as a useful distraction, and planned the—um—operation against Limbert accordingly. But that's extremely unlikely. The thing was almost certainly pure coincidence. Not that that's an end of the matter. You see, between midnight, when our people took up their positions, and somewhere round about two o'clock, when the raid, or fiasco, or whatever it's to be called, was all over, nobody could have stirred in the streets round about here without having to give an account of himself. I needn't go into the whole topography now, sir; you may simply take that as a fact. And it suggests that, as far as the Limbert drama was concerned, the whole set-up was complete by midnight. And that it was then confined within these walls until two o'clock or thereabouts."

"Sort of sealed room."

"Something like that. And perhaps rather unnerving for the criminals, if there were any. Suddenly discovering, I mean, that for some inexplicable reason the whole district was stiff with police."

"What about activity on that fire-escape?"

"I've looked into that. Anybody leaving the yard below would have been spotted, as long as our people were on the job. But I can't find that the escape itself was under observation. Everything too dark on that side of the house. People may have been hopping up and down it, and in and out of windows for that matter, all through the night. And of course up and down the inside staircase as well."

"And along the roofs?"

"The roofs are out. There's a possible route from above the Thomas Carlyle along the Gas Street roofs, so we had a couple of men up there. They'd have seen any funny business."

"Dear me." Appleby was mildly astonished. "What odd things go on in the Force nowadays. Men lurking on roofs to catch expensive people drinking bad champagne in cellars. How very thorough."

"The roof notion was her ladyship's. Talking of cellars, there's quite a handsome one here. You get at it from under the stairs. No other way out—not even a coalhole—but it would be quite a good spot for anybody wanting to lurk."

"Like the fellow Grace Brooks talks of. By the way, what about the other girl in the picture—the one upstairs. When was she discovered to have vanished?"

"Mary Arrow. As you can see, Limbert had a telephone—there it is in the corner. The constable got on to his station at once, and there was another man here in no time. One of them went all over the house to see what was what. Miss Arrow was out. Bed not slept in, and breakfast either not eaten or completely cleared away. Door unlocked. And she just didn't come back. When it began to look odd the local people found a bosom friend of hers a couple of streets away. This girl had a look round, and swore that Miss Arrow had taken nothing away with her except the clothes on her back. Tweeds."

"Not even a tooth-brush?"

Cadover stared. "I don't know that they looked into that."

"In novels people setting off on an unpremeditated adventure commonly snatch up a tooth-brush. A thoroughly unlikely proceeding which novel-reading might nevertheless actually induce. We'll have a look."

"Yes, sir—of course." Of this, his chief's first positive suggestion in the Limbert affair, Cadover did not appear to think highly. "We inquired into Miss Arrow's background. Nothing there. But she has people to whom she is in the habit of writing home every three or four days. They've had nothing from her to date."

"That doesn't look good."

"That's what it will presently be necessary to admit to them."

"And Limbert's background?"

"Army people. Parents both dead; no brothers or sisters; plenty of uncles and aunts. Boy had an impeccable past. All the usual inquiries made for a lad of that class: local vicar, housemaster, tutor at Cambridge, respectable people to whom he had introductions while studying in Paris. Nothing."

"Nothing will come of nothing."

"There's always a wise word in Shakespeare, no doubt." Cadover had gone back to the Stubbs. "This oughtn't to be left here, if it's really valuable. Limbert left no will, but a family solicitor has turned up and proposes to settle his affairs. We're responsible to him, as long as we keep a key of this place."

"Then we'll take the Stubbs away with us." Appleby crossed the room, took down the picture, and glanced at the wall behind it. "Can we get in to this Mary Arrow's flat?"

Cadover nodded. "I've got a key in my pocket."

"Then we'll take a glance at that before closing down for the night."

The apartments of the missing woman corresponded exactly to those of Limbert below. They had an air of spaciousness proceeding from the circumstance that they contained almost nothing except a bed and a grand piano. There was a drawing of a female torso by Limbert on the wall. Appleby paused before it. "I don't suppose you know whether this represents Miss Arrow?"

"How could I? It hasn't even got a head." Cadover was exasperated. "I suppose they start with bodies, because they're easier to do. But we have photographs of the girl, if you're interested."

"Good looking?"

"I suppose she would be called that."

"She certainly lives the simple life." Appleby had moved to a narrow shelf near the bed. "Spartan plainness all round—except for these things."

"These little pots and bottles?" Cadover looked suspiciously at the shelf.

"Cosmetics—and just those considered basically necessary. But of their kind, very good indeed."

"Expensive?"

"My dear man—what do you suppose? And now for the bathroom. Thirty years on the job doesn't make one quite comfortable about this sort of snooping. Do you remember the death of Hardy's Mrs Henchard? 'And all her shining keys will be took from her, and her cupboards opened; and little things a' didn't wish seen, anybody will see.' It has often haunted me, when nosing around. . . . I thought so. No toothbrush."

Cadover came to the bathroom door. "No toothbrush?"

"She must have had one. A girl doesn't spend all that on cosmetics and then fail to clean her teeth. But look for yourself. Mug, yes. Brush, no."

Cadover's fingers went to his jaw. "Perhaps she has dentures, and just soaks them in something."

"Nonsense. There's an empty tube of ordinary toothpaste there on the window-sill. I really think there's no doubt about it. She thought 'I'm going after this, and I don't know when I'll be back.' And at that— being a novel-reader, as I said—she picked up the tooth-brush and dropped it into her handbag. Can you see any other explanation?"

Before taking up this challenge, Cadover stooped down and peered under the bath. "Yes," he said. "I can. The brush may have been taken by another person in order to induce the supposition you have arrived at."

"An ingenious suggestion—but one also belonging

51

to the world of the novel, if you ask me. I'm going to suppose that the missing tooth-brush tells us quite a lot. That the girl didn't simply go out in a normal way, get knocked down by a bus, and for some reason elude identification in hospital. That she wasn't, on the other hand, kidnapped by criminals. That she was persuaded—or perhaps merely persuaded herself—to go off in a great hurry, possibly in some spirit of adventure, and with the expectation of being absent from this flat for at least one night. Had she a valid passport?"

"Yes."

"Currency?"

"She got thirty pounds in traveller's cheques a few months ago, and they were all cashed in France a week later. She might have brought enough back in francs to go abroad with again. No other transactions of that sort since, and none of her ordinary cheques have turned up at her bank since she vanished. Incidentally, I didn't inquire about the state of her account. But I was given a hint that it was in a perfectly healthy state. All this austerity, and breakfasting off a moonlight sonata"—Cadover, as he permitted himself this unwontedly picturesque expression, gestured at the grand piano—"was a matter of principle, I rather gather. Father is a Rural Dean. But the mother has money. And—talking about money—there's another thing. We found a small strongbox in a drawer over there, unlocked and left open. There was nothing in it but a little Italian money—a couple of thousand-lire notes. So she may have wrapped whatever else was there round that tooth-brush. Would you say a novel-reader would do that?"

Appleby smiled. "Decidedly. Do you mean the

strongbox was in that chest of drawers in the corner?"

"Yes."

"Go on looking at it. Don't look towards the south window. There's somebody reconnoitring us from the fire-escape."

"Is there, indeed?" Cadover contrived to remain staring at the chest in a most convincing brown study.

"I'll do something intriguing. Meanwhile you slip downstairs and get on the escape through Limbert's window. That will fix him."

Cadover nodded and drifted towards the door. Appleby dropped to his knees and went through the motions of one who picks fine hairs off the pile of a carpet. He brought a matchbox from his pocket and appeared to tuck something away in it. When he judged a suitable interval to have elapsed he got up and walked straight towards the window. A head disappeared as he did so. He threw up the sash and peered out. At the same moment Cadover emerged upon the iron structure from the window below, just recognisable in the dusk. The intruder, thus neatly caught in the process of scurrying towards ground level, instantly sat down on one of the steps, produced and lit a cigarette, and gazed into the surrounding void with the air of a man meditating at leisure upon the mutability of human affairs.

"Good evening." Appleby spoke drily from above—but to no effect. The philosopher of the fire-escape continued to muse.

"Now then—you there. What are you up to?"

This was Cadover's more brusque address from below. The abstracted stranger could be discerned as moving his head slightly, and vaguely scanning surrounding space, as if uncertain whether he had not been addressed by some celestial visitant.

"You can go up or you can go down. We want to have a look at you."

Cadover's voice, now loud and menacing, appeared to persuade the ruminative figure of what was the lesser of two evils before him. He got to his feet and climbed. "A mild night," he said. He contrived to give this statement the air of pure soliloquy. "How pleasant to step out upon this convenient stairway and smoke a cigarette." He paused, like a man surrounded only by a great loneliness, and well pleased with his own company. "Yes, indeed. It is an amenity which you are fortunate to enjoy, my dear fellow. . . . Dear me—I had no idea!" He started elaborately as his glance met Appleby's. "Good evening. I fancied I was quite alone."

"No doubt." Appleby drew back. "Perhaps you'll come inside?"

The stranger climbed in, and was presently followed by Cadover. The latter eyed him grimly. "So it's you, Mr Zhitkov. I rather thought it was."

"Good evening, Colonel." Zhitkov was a foreigner who spoke fluent but slightly erratic English. "How do you do, reverend sir." He had turned to Appleby. "We are all here much distressed about your daughter. It is an anxiety to us. She was in my thoughts only a few moments ago, when I stepped out for a breath of this delightful evening air." Whether from fright, or because the delightful evening air was of decidedly wintry temper, Zhitkov's teeth were chattering slightly.

"I am not Miss Arrow's father." Appleby much doubted whether he had really been taken for a Rural

54

Dean. "Like Inspector Cadover, I belong to the police. You were peering in on us a moment ago."

"Can I have done that?" Zhitkov's manner was that of a man presented with some impersonal observation of minor scientific interest. "It was my impression that I had not climbed so high. But no doubt I had. I was in deep thought, you will understand, over a technical problem."

"We're doing a little deep thinking over a technical problem ourselves. Perhaps you can assist us." Appleby turned to Cadover. "What account does this gentleman give of his movements during the material times?"

"In his studio, he says, on the ground floor. Alone. No witnesses."

"And perhaps now and then taking a breath or two of night air on the fire-escape—of course without noticing?"

Zhitkov made as if to speak, thought better of it, and took a quick, nervous puff at his cigarette. He was a small man in late middle-age, dressed in old, carefully tended, somewhat formal clothes. Although his situation was disadvantageous and his manner patently disingenuous, he gave no suggestion of impudence. He had, in fact, an air of breeding—or of what is left of breeding when it has for long been played upon by an unstable or shiftless temperament. One met such people on the fringes of the great ballet companies. Appleby put him down, provisionally, as some sort of Slavonic *emigré* of long standing. "Mr Zhitkov," he said, "I understand that you are a sculptor?"

"I carve. And I model, experimentally, in several new mediums."

"It is your living?"

Zhitkov hesitated. "I do a certain amount of commercial work. In wax."

Cadover was interested in this. "Do you mean the sort of things in shop-windows?" he demanded. "I thought they were done from moulds."

"I do a little of that. The demand now is often for figures so stylised that it is useless to take moulds from the life."

"I never knew that. And waxworks for fun-fairs, and so on?"

Zhitkov shrugged his shoulders. "And that too," he said, rather coldly. "*C'est mon deuxième métier*. That is something which few artists avoid nowadays."

"That's very true, unfortunately." Appleby's manner was now amiable. "By the way, Mr Zhitkov, did Gavin Limbert have a *deuxième métier*?"

"I think not. In his family were *les gens riches*. So he was not constrained to it."

"No copying, for instance—or doing stuff in the manner of the old masters for the American market?"

"Nothing of the sort."

"I know that there are a good many ways in which an artist can get mixed up in funny business with some profit to himself. Nothing of that sort?"

Zhitkov's eyelids flickered. It was almost as if a new—and disconcerting—idea had been presented to him. "I know of nothing."

"You may have heard that this afternoon, during the private view at the Da Vinci, a painting of Limbert's was stolen——"

"*What?*" Zhitkov's cigarette dropped to the floor, and his eyes had dilated. "Not the—not his last painting? . . . *stolen?*"

56

"Definitely his last painting. You know it, Mr Zhitkov?"

"I saw Limbert at work on it once or twice. It was most interesting." Zhitkov had very much the appearance of a man trying hard to regain control of his nerves. "A wonderful work."

"You consider that Limbert was a promising young painter?"

"Certainly. He would have been a great painter. We are all in deep sorrow at his death."

"This final painting of his—the one that has been stolen. Would you say that it was his masterpiece, and well worth stealing?"

Zhitkov hesitated —and Appleby wondered if it was really in the interest of a sound aesthetic judgment. "But assuredly. It was in a new manner. Limbert had done nothing quite like it before. The tones were remarkable. It was what we call a painter's picture. Doubtless it has been stolen on the instructions of some unscrupulous collector."

"Wouldn't it have been easier to buy it? I doubt whether the Da Vinci would have stuck out for a very large figure, though they would talk big at first. It seems unlikely that any substantial collector, however unscrupulous, would put himself in the power of a criminal agent, and moreover make it impossible that he should ever display his Limbert, simply for the sake of a few score of guineas. I think, Mr Zhitkov, that here is a technical problem upon which your thought hasn't been quite so deep as it might be."

This time Zhitkov blinked, and Appleby had the sense of a man thinking hard. But when he spoke it was politely and indifferently. "It is a point," he said. "You may well be right."

57

"And now about Miss Arrow, whose flat this is. Her disappearance is undoubtedly strange. And it coincided, of course, with the death of Limbert. Have you any opinion on how these two events may be connected?"

"She may have killed him."

"Quite so. Would it be a surprise to you if that did, in fact, turn out to be the explanation?"

"It would be a sorrow." Zhitkov looked frigidly at Cadover, from whom this sentiment had drawn a grunt of impatience. "The world is so murderously inclined to artists that it is a great distress to see them murdering one another."

Appleby looked hard at the sculptor. "Were you ever aware of Limbert and Miss Arrow quarrelling?"

"Miss Arrow was not a person who would conduct quarrels in public."

"And Limbert?"

"He would quarrel, quite cheerfully, if he found occasion to."

"With you?"

"Yes, Limbert was very unpleasant to me more than once. But—how do you put it—without rancour. When I have had parties, and some of my friends have been noisy late into the night, Limbert has been very rude. But it was nothing."

"Did you hear him quarrelling with anyone on the day of his death?"

"No. But then I was absent from my studio on business during the greater part of the day. There may have been such a quarrel."

"There was—or at least there was a dispute. It appears that some man presented himself to Limbert, making what he called a fair offer. Limbert seems to have suggested that his visitor was a bit of a crook. His visitor then threatened to invoke the law, saying that some transaction or other had not, in fact, been a valid purchase. . . . You are interested in this?"

Zhitkov had momentarily the appearance of being very much interested; he had gone quite tense, and was staring at Appleby with glittering eyes. But immediately he relaxed again. "I am naturally interested. This, you say, was on the day of Limbert's death. It may be important."

"I agree with you. Then Limbert turned this person out. I have as yet no idea who he might be. Perhaps you can help me there. The fellow is said, incidentally, to have hung about Gas Street for most of the rest of the day. "

Zhitkov shook his head. "I can be of no help. But if anything occurs to me, of course I shall let you know." His eyes strayed to the door, and Appleby felt that he was in some sudden anxiety that the interview should end. "I live at the bottom, as you know. And I can be found at any time."

"I am sure you can." Appleby's tone was urbane but significant. "We shall certainly have no difficulty, Mr Zhitkov, in looking you up if we find it necessary. But in the meantime we must not detain you further."

"Will you go by the staircase, or would you prefer a little more evening air on the fire-escape?"

But upon Cadover, thus lumbering up with his heaviest irony, Zhitkov wasted very little time. "Thank you, Colonel," he murmured vaguely. "You are too kind." And with a stiff bow he marched from the room.

*   *   *

Cadover looked at his watch. "You'll be late for dinner." His tone might have been taken as adding, "And don't blame me if there's a row."

"Then come along. We'll take Limbert's Stubbs into safe-keeping, and lock up both these flats. Isn't there another storey, by the way? The fire-escape seems to go up further."

Cadover nodded. "There's a single big attic room. Not much more than a loft, and empty at present. But another possible place for lurking."

"I see." Appleby had moved out to the little landing and was peering up the final dusty flight of stairs. "Nasty little warren this place is, from our point of view. Anybody able to hop in on anybody else—and out again by that fire-escape. Well, I've seen for myself. And I'll spend tomorrow morning on the file."

"We must get them on to that girl Brooks's story." Cadover had now possessed himself of the Stubbs and was making all secure in Limbert's studio. "The fellow with whom there was that row is just as likely a suspect as Miss Arrow." Cadover again looked at his watch. "Better run you home first, I suppose. It will save you five minutes. May make all the difference to the soup."

"Very well. But I sometimes wonder what makes you envisage my domestic life as such a tyranny." Appleby sniffed as they reached the ground floor. "Boxer's having another fry."

"I have my doubts about that man." Cadover was frowning as they climbed into the big police car. "Very improper, his having tried to dissuade the girl from telling her story. . . . I'll put this painting on the seat between us, if you don't mind. Wouldn't do to kick a hole in it." Cadover set the Stubbs down gingerly; it was evidently an anxiety to him. "Yes, very improper, indeed."

"Possibly so." Appleby put a hand on the picture as the car swung into King's Road. "But it can't be called suspicious. Boxer just doesn't much believe in having people chased by the police—not even murderers. He is probably inclined to philosophic anarchism. Many of those people are."

"So much the worse. If he feels anarchistic about Limbert dead, he may have felt anarchistic about him alive. I'm not inclined to rule out Boxer. Nor Zhitkov either. Most suspicious, the way he came snooping up that escape when we were in Miss Arrow's room. Of course"—Cadover was firmly judicial—"it may have been no more than vulgar curiosity. Like the kids who were gaping at this car when we came out."

Appleby shook his head. "I don't think Zhitkov would have much impulse to be vulgarly curious. He had some more substantial motive for that little reconnaissance. You know, I think there's a good deal buried in this affair. And I have a feeling that at one point you had pretty well got at it."

"*I* had got at it?" Cadover was astonished. "I'm afraid I don't feel at all that way myself."

"There was a point at which you said something extremely relevant to the whole puzzle. Only it has escaped me. . . . But here I am." The car had come to a halt just as Big Ben, from not far away, chimed eight o'clock. "Look after the Stubbs." Appleby leant forward and opened the door of the car.

But Cadover was looking dubiously at the picture. The notion of a valuable painting was one which he appeared to find obstinately mysterious and oppressive. "You know, sir, we gave no receipt. It's a bit irregular, come to think of it. I wonder if you'd mind taking the responsibility yourself?"

Appleby laughed. "Not in the least. I've got a fire-proof safe that will just hold it. And I'll bring it to the Yard in the morning and see that it's properly accounted for myself. We'll meet at nine o'clock and go over the whole affair. Good night." And Appleby got out of the car, mounted the steps of his quiet Westminster house, and let himself in at the front door.

Judith, it seemed, hadn't waited. From the dining-room came the sound of a meal in progress. Appleby, with the Stubbs still under his arm, crossed the hall and entered. Dinner—dinner for two—was certainly going on; it had reached the stage of mutton chops. Judith was wearing her old Worth black and her pearls. And the reason for this was immediately apparent. Her companion was the Duke of Horton.

"There, my dear—you were wrong. And I've eaten the poor fellow's chop. Such a particularly good chop, too." The Duke had risen—vague, in every sense ancient, wholly unperturbed—and shaken Appleby's hand. "Your wife was positive that if you weren't in by a quarter to eight it must be taken for granted you had gone to your club."

"Quite right, sir. It's a family rule." Appleby managed to smile with equal urbanity both at his guest and his wife. "And I'm glad to see Judith found the Mouton-Rothschild 'twenty-nine."

"Yes, indeed—a remarkable wine. I have been appreciating it keenly." The Duke's glance went hurriedly over the table. Presumably he had been unaware of the claret, and felt that it must be located if this civil protestation were to be rendered convincing. "In spite of this vexatious business being so much on my mind. Or rather on Anne's mind." Anne was the Duchess of Horton. "Anne sent me up to town about it. She said that the time for action had come, and she advised me to go straight to you. Reminded me of what you had done for us at the time of the Auldearn affair. So when I failed to get you at that great police place off Whitehall I decided I'd come along here later. Been boring Lady Appleby, I'm afraid, with the whole tiresome thing."

"Your goldfish and silverfish and aquarium?" Appleby put the Stubbs down on a chair, and contrived to advance with every appearance of pleasurable anticipation upon the remains of a tinned ham.

"Yes, my dear fellow—yes, indeed. A shocking loss. You remember those rascals who went round thieving things in the last years of the war, and who got our Titian? Called themselves by some damned impudent name. Beg your pardon, m'dear."

"The International Society for the Diffusion of Cultural Objects?"

"That was it. Well, Anne thinks it must be a similar gang of scoundrels who are at work now."

"I don't quite see why the Duchess should think that." Appleby, who had sat down and helped himself cheerfully to mustard, was perplexed. "Would thieves like that really take goldfish and silverfish——"

Judith burst out laughing. "John is quite as much at sea as the fish."

"I've failed to make myself clear." The Duke of Horton's eye was solicitously on Appleby's plate; having eaten his chop, he now appeared to regard himself as in something of the position of host. "My dear man—let me reach you that salad from the side." He

63

set down his claret with what was now impeccable respect, got to his feet, and at once dumbfounded the Applebys by emitting an altogether unducal yell. Moved by a common impulse, they peered under the table. The only possible explanation of their guest's bizarre behaviour seemed to be that he had been bitten by an intrusive family pet. But nothing canine was visible. When they looked up again it was to see the Duke staring incredulously at the Stubbs.

"But, my dear Appleby, this is superb. You have excelled yourself—which is to say a great deal." Momentarily abandoning the picture, the Duke advanced upon Appleby and took him warmly by the hand. "It was only a few hours ago that I reported the theft at your office, and here already is one of the pictures safe and sound."

"One of the *pictures*?" Mechanically Appleby reached for the claret bottle. "You've been talking about *pictures*?"

"Goldfish and Silverfish—the two finest horses my great-grandfather ever had. That *is* my great-grandfather, sitting in the curricle. And the fellow at Silverfish's head is Morgan, his favourite groom. Stubbs, you know, was brought into notice by the Duke of Richmond. Keen rival of Richmond's, was my great-grandfather. And I've always liked the painting, I'm bound to say. Quite apart from the fact that old Stubbs is now rather a swell." The Duke paused. "You wouldn't, my dear chap, have recovered the other one too? We're uncommonly anxious about it. After all, George Stubbs is one thing. But Jan——"

"I've been an ass." Appleby, comically disconcerted, turned to his wife. "Judith, I *have* been an ass?"

Judith was serious again. "I don't know about that. But by the aquarium the Duke means what you think. Vermeer's Aquarium. The greatest picture at Scamnum Court."

4

"Times have changed down our way." It was half an hour later, and in a large bubble of glass the Duke of Horton was slowly rotating a tot from Appleby's last bottle of old brandy. "A great bus station at King's Horton on the ground where we used to go over and light their bonfires on big occasions. And two tea gardens in Scamnum Ducis, both out to capture our own trade."

"Your own trade?" Judith was puzzled.

"Dear me, yes. We do teas in the Orangery. Had them catered at first. But then Anne took it over herself and has made a very good thing of it. Important part of the museum business, it seems. And we're in that right up to the neck. Open every day of the year, except Good Friday. Miles of mud-proof matting through all the rooms and down all the corridors. People go through by the thousands, at half-a-crown a head."

"How very restless." Judith was sympathetic. "Do they do a lot of damage?"

"No, no—nothing of the kind. Very decent people, and often extremely interested. I get quite a lot of intelligent questions."

Appleby was looking for cigars. "You take parties through yourself, sir?"

"We both do. It didn't seem civil to open the old place up in that fashion and not take a hand in doing the honours ourselves. Anne feels the same about her tea-shop. She often drops in and carries round a tray. But you were asking about damage. Charity balls are the fatal thing there. Let in a lot of opulent Yahoos at ten guineas a time and they feel entitled to break up the whole place. Treat your carpets as if they were on board one of those horrible great liners. But the half-a-crowners are a very respectable kind of folk. Very quiet. And the more they see, the quieter they get."

"I expect it's a pretty overwhelming two-and-sixpence worth."

The Duke looked at the cigars now being held out to him. "You think so?" he said doubtfully. "They vary, of course. But I find a lot of Jamaicas not at all bad."

Appleby smiled. "Then try them. But I was meaning the tour of Scamnum Court, as a matter of fact."

"To be sure." The Duke was not at all put out. "Well, I dare say we give as good value as most. Blenheim, for instance. You may say it offers rather more historical interest than we do. But you have to remember it's not half the size. Friend of mine says we ought to make a two-day affair of it, and earn a bit more by putting people up for the night. But the half-crowns do well enough. Put us rather in the category of being in the entertainment business and running at a loss. Helpful."

"I suppose so." Appleby nodded. "But not if it leads to your losing a Vermeer every now and then—or even a Stubbs. I hope the pictures were insured against the increased risk from all this new traffic?"

"I've a very good man sees to all that. Insisted on the thing when I rather jibbed at the premium. The Vermeer's insured for what my poor father gave for it. But of course I could sell it back to America for three times as much as that."

"Ever thought of doing so?"

"Anne wouldn't let me. I believe she'd rather part with the little Rembrandt thunder-storm—the one her father bought in Dublin for ten shillings. And she prizes that almost as much as he did."

"I think the Duchess is quite right." Judith had crossed the room to a book-case, and now returned with a monograph on Vermeer, open at a reproduction of the stolen painting. "It seems unbelievable that it's gone; that it's even in danger, perhaps, of destruction."

"I feel very bad about it." The Duke, who had decided to finish his brandy before essaying the cigar, settled back with every appearance of mellowed comfort in his chair. "Upbringing, you know. I was taught that we simply held all those things in trust. Not for the nation. My father disapproved of nations, whether his own or any other. But for civilisation in general. So in losing the Vermeer I feel that I've fallen down, rather, on the job. And Anne is fearfully upset. She has a thing about it." The Duke, conscious that with this colloquialism he was indulging the young people before him with their own most modish jargon, amiably smiled.

"The Duchess has a thing about holding things in trust?"

"Bless me, no. Anne was brought up much more sensibly than I was. Anne has a thing about the Vermeer—about the Aquarium. She calls it the luck of the Crispins."

Judith lit a cigarette. "But it hasn't been with the Crispins long enough for that, surely. Your father bought it in New York."

"Very true. But Anne's point is that the Aquarium is a sort of Crispin conversation piece. These fantastically bred, brightly coloured little creatures, like so many jewels in a transparent casket, and in a world so utterly of their own: Anne says that's us. We'll last, she says, as long as we keep up the show; as long as we go on swimming confidently behind the enchanted glass."

Appleby was looking at the reproduction over his wife's shoulder. "The Duchess is quite right. The half-crowns are never further from stringing you up on a lamp-post than when they've just had their money's worth of Scamnum's intolerable splendours. But now, perhaps, if you wouldn't mind——"

"Yes, yes, my dear fellow—to be sure. Remarkable brandy this. I have nothing like it." For the first time, the Duke of Horton appeared slightly uncomfortable. "This happened three weeks ago. And you want to know why I've kept it dark. I'm wondering, by the way, if we can keep *that* dark—I mean about this delay in telling the police, and the insurance people, and the papers. Say we hadn't noticed . . . something of that sort. But not, of course, if you think not."

"I think not." Appleby shook his head with every appearance of judicial consideration. "When really valuable property is in question, no subterfuge is exactly harmless."

"No doubt you're right." The Duke sighed. "Of course you can guess what the trouble was. It might have been a member of the family."

"Quite so." Detective investigation among the upper classes had long accustomed Appleby to the smooth navigating of this particular stretch of troubled water. "But fortunately any fear of that sort has proved groundless."

The Duke brightened. "Groundless—exactly. Or *probably* groundless. At the time, I had doubts about my nephew, Miles. Since we sold up in Morayshire, you know, his father has done little more than drift about, waiting for me to die. And Miles comes and stops with us quite a lot."

"Is that the Master of Kincrae?" Judith had rather the air of turning over the pages of an invisible *Who's Who*.

"Yes, yes—young Miles. I've always thought the Scottish titles a bit of an affectation with people like ourselves." The Duke was politely impatient. "And Miles, you see, knows a lot about art. So we thought of him at once."

"I see." Judith, less familiar with this territory than her husband, was mildly disconcerted by such facility of intra-familial suspicion.

"And then there's my sister Grace. She lives by herself in the East Gate-house and insists on having keys to almost everything. It's not possible to refuse her anything of that sort. Because, you know, she's temperamental, and might do something really awkward if thwarted. You see?"

"Yes—of course." Judith was a little doubtful about the wisdom of humouring Grace in just this way.

"And Grace does sometimes—um—move things about oddly. It's only a couple of years since she managed to abstract the church plate from the safe in our poor vicar's vestry, and stow it away in a cupboard in a disused milking-parlour on the home farm. It was an eccentric thing to do—although no doubt her action had some basis in theological conviction. The habit would be less vexatious in a smaller building. But at Scamnum there are so many places where things can be stowed away. It's one of my reasons for sometimes wishing I lived in a smaller house. Like this, for instance. So snug."

And the Duke lit his cigar. Appleby watched him thoughtfully. "The fact that the Stubbs has turned up in London seems to put Lady Grace's type of activity out of account. And you're sure about Miles?"

"Pretty sure. The more I've thought about it, the more certain I've become that it couldn't be any member of the family. The fact is, it was a theft with brains behind it. But you must judge of that for yourself. I'll simply tell you how we've come to think it must have been done. Unless you feel there's some action you should be taking first?"

Appleby shook his head. "I did a little telephoning while you were finishing your coffee. And it's likely that there will be one or two callers presently. But meanwhile, please carry on."

"First about the dates, then." The Duke of Horton put down his cigar and fished out a pocket diary. "Yes, here we are. On Sunday, the 14th of October, both

72

the Vermeer and the Stubbs were safe and sound."

Appleby made a note. It took somebody like his present visitor, he was reflecting, to spend nearly three weeks quietly sitting on the theft of one of the world's great pictures.

"The Aquarium, of course, hangs in the picture gallery in the east wing. The place is like the strong-room of a bank nowadays. There are steel lattices that draw over the doors and windows—and even over the two Alfred Stevens' fireplaces—at night. The key comes to me—or to my old butler, Bagot, if I'm away from Scamnum—and later it's collected by the watch-man when he comes on duty. We get along with one man going round at night."

"Reliable?"

"Getting on in years, but absolutely trustworthy—my batman, as a matter of fact, in the Kaiser's war."

"Does Lady Grace have a key to the picture gallery?"

"No. It's about the only place she doesn't have the run of in that way. I really think you can quite count her out."

"I think so too."

"Well, now, on that Sunday Anne happened to have down a great nob in the art line—nice little German from Munich. We took him to one part of the house and another during the course of the afternoon—between parties, of course."

"Between parties of half-crowners?"

"Exactly so. A party starts off every half-hour. But we've learnt to dodge about between them—make rather a game of it, as a matter of fact. Well, of course, we took this fellow to the picture gallery, and the Aquarium was there, safe enough. Chap went over every square inch of it, muttering about the technique, and the *pintamenti*, and things of that sort."

"What about the Stubbs?"

"That doesn't hang in the gallery, but in a small room opening off it, that we don't show. I have a fancy for doing my accounts there on a Sunday morning, and it has half-a-dozen things like the Stubbs—things that I'm particularly fond of. So I happen to know that the Stubbs was safe that morning too. And now we move on to Wednesday." The Duke turned the page of his diary, with the effect of placidly enjoying his own efficiency. "On the Wednesday afternoon a chap called Morgan sought me out in a bit of a dither. Son of my present steward, and a descendant of the fellow holding Goldfish and Silverfish in the picture there. He's one of the four people regularly employed in taking the half-a-crowners round. Having been brought up about the place he has a good command of the sort of patter they like. Well, he said he thought there was something wrong with the Vermeer. I went up to the gallery at once. It was a dull afternoon, and for a moment I couldn't myself see that there was anything amiss. Then I tumbled to it. What was in the frame wasn't the Vermeer at all. It was a colour print—the full-size one I authorised a couple of years ago. And the damned thing—beg pardon, m'dear—was almost indetectable. People had been gaping at it all day as the veritable masterpiece itself. Smart, eh?"

Judith Appleby picked up her book again. "Particularly smart with a Vermeer. No knobbly *impasto*. Surface like enamel. But what about the Stubbs?"

"They couldn't play the same trick with that, because it has never been reproduced in any form. And, in fact, it had simply been taken out of its frame, and then off its stretcher."

"There's something odd about that." Appleby got up and paced about the room. "And why wasn't it missed earlier?"

"I've explained that to you. Nobody goes into that little room, except myself on Sunday mornings, and somebody who cleans it on Fridays. The chap who shuts up for the night just glances in."

"What about that night-watchman?"

"He flicks on the lights and takes a glance around. But the Stubbs was rather tucked away behind a screen. And, of course, he can't scrutinise every room in Scamnum. It would take him a week."

Appleby nodded. "It looks as if the Vermeer was taken by means of an elaborately prepared plan; and as if the Stubbs was a bit of an afterthought by somebody tolerably well acquainted with the habits of the household. It was the last point that made you uneasy, no doubt."

"Quite so. And that's pretty well the whole story. But as you're bound, my dear fellow, to have a lot of questions to ask, I'll just take a little more of that brandy. My cousin Gervase has a very good brandy— but, I assure you, nothing like this."

"I remember the picture gallery very well. It doesn't offer any hiding place?"

"Nothing of the sort."

"But what about that little room opening off it?"

"It's no more than a cupboard. No possibility there either."

"Not behind that screen you spoke about?"

"Dear me, no. And remember that lurking intruders are just what the watchman has in mind all the time. The local police set tremendous stress on it. They say nobody breaks into a big house who can just walk in and hide."

"Clearly they're right. Do you make a count of the half-crowners as they come and go?"

"We can't manage that. One of them might very well lurk in the house overnight. But, as I've said, not in the picture gallery."

"About the Aquarium: was its stretcher found too?"

"No. It had gone. And the colour print had simply been glued to the back of the frame."

"I see." Appleby turned to Judith. "What about taking a fair-sized painting like that off its stretcher and rolling it up?"

"It could be done. But at some risk. Nobody would do it if they could possibly help it."

"I thought about it's being got out of the picture gallery." The Duke nodded sagely. "And it could be done without rolling it up, simply by feeding it out of the window and having it caught by somebody down below. Because there is one window at the end that is like that—not lattice, just permanent upright bars."

"Then that's how it took its departure." Appleby had sat down again. "Was anything suspicious noticed about any of the visitors during the two or three days when the thing may have happened? I'm afraid it's rather a vague question."

"I've made inquiries about that." The Duke was again pleased with himself. "It seems that there was one fellow—he was on his own—who came a couple of days running. It was Morgan again who remembered him. He was lame and had to go around with a stick. Usually, you see, we ask people to leave any sticks or umbrellas behind them when they come in.

But this chap, of course, was allowed to hobble round on his. That was what made Morgan notice him both times—the last party on Sunday afternoon, and then one of the first on Monday morning."

Appleby nodded. "It rather looks as if we're hot on the scent. Was this chap actually seen to leave on Sunday, or to arrive on the following morning?"

"I gather not. There are tremendous mobs, you know. And Morgan just noticed him each time in the course of his round."

"He sounds just the man we want. It's particularly significant that he was lame."

"Is that so?" The Duke was impressed. "Celebrated limping criminal who steals pictures and is known to the police?"

"Not exactly that. Judith, what's the size of the Aquarium?"

"It's one of the few big ones—big, that is, for Vermeer. You might call it five feet by four."

"Then we may be pretty sure that the colour print entered Scamnum Court done in a roll down that fellow's trouser-leg. He *had* to be lame, and hobble along with a stiff leg. It's all clear enough, except how he got into the picture gallery, or managed to spend the night there. Not that there's more than academic interest in that."

"But he might do it again." The Duke set down the stub of his cigar in alarm. "He might take the Rembrandt or the Gainsborough. Except, of course, that I've now put in a man to guard the place all night. But it's a nasty feeling. Unknown secret passages in one's own house—that sort of thing. But they weren't a feature of Kent's building."

Appleby shook his head. "I don't think the thief

77

found a secret passage. Have there been any changes in the picture gallery lately in the way of furniture and so on?"

"It's just as you remember it. Nothing in it at all, except rows of pictures on the walls, and bronzes and marbles in the niches, and a line of those shallow display cabinets, and a useless Louis Quatorze chair in each window. Oh, and there's the Spanish chest that the nice old boy Leoni sent Anne."

"Who is Leoni?"

"Good chap. Old Italian family." The Duke of Horton, whose own ancestors had appeared from nowhere in the time of Henry VIII, had a great respect for ancient lineage. "He was rather awkwardly placed here for a time during the war, and Anne sorted things out. Charming of him to send her this whopping great Spanish chest. Remembered all about Scamnum too. Asked particularly that the thing should stand in the picture gallery, under the Velasquez. Man with fine taste in that sort of thing."

"When did this chest arrive?"

"About a month ago. Sent from Rome."

"And the Duchess wrote acknowledging it?"

"Naturally, my dear fellow. She wrote off at once to Leoni, with inquiries about his family and that sort of thing. But she's had no reply from him so far."

"Well, I'm blessed." Appleby regarded the Duke with astonishment. "You remember when the Duchess got up her performance of *Hamlet* at Scamnum?"

"Never likely to forget it." The Duke turned to Judith. "Occasion of my meeting your husband for the first time. Shocking things happened—perfectly shocking. But I don't see——"

Appleby smiled. "I think the Duchess should now

have a go at *Cymbeline*. It might teach her to distrust charming Italians anxious to have large chests deposited in particular apartments."

For a moment the Duke stared at Appleby open-mouthed. "I quite see what you mean. But, dash it all, Leoni——"

"He may know nothing about it. The Duchess has had no reply to her letter of thanks, and the address to which she wrote may well have been a fake one. This chest would hold a man comfortably?"

"I suppose it would. But isn't this a bit far fetched, my dear chap? We know positively that the Spanish chest is rather a fine piece. It must be worth three or four hundred pounds. Would anybody——"

"Your Vermeer is worth thirty or forty thousand even in the limited market of mad collectors. And the chest's being valuable made you feel that your Italian friend had been extremely generous, and that made you the more certain to accept the suggestion that it should be placed in the picture gallery. So there it was, a ready-made hiding place. The lame fellow watched his chance on the Sunday afternoon and nipped inside it. Just like Iachimo, except that he wasn't positively carried into position by sweating porters. Then he did his job in the small hours, dropped the Aquarium through the window bars to a confederate, took a prowl around and saw that he could safely take the Stubbs for luck, got into the chest again before opening time, and joined the first crowd being shown through in the morning. It could be done easily enough when the half-crowners were being harangued before a picture."

"But why was he lame the second time?" It was Judith who asked the question. "He'd got rid of the rolled-up print. So there was no need of it."

"He was still the same chap who had been through the day before—and in the same clothes. If he was recognised, and spotted as walking normally, somebody might begin wondering why. It was all very well thought out."

"Decidedly so." The Duke looked slightly dazed. "And the astonishing thing is that you've solved the mystery while just sitting there. And, of course, recovered the Stubbs already. If you could just——"

"I'm not without hopes. If the worst comes to the worst, we can work at the thing from the other end. Of course most of the people who will pay big money for stolen masterpieces live in America, and coming up with them would take time. So we must try to put our hands on the Aquarium while it remains in this country. For that, time is important. Tomorrow may be too late. But the Aquarium certainly isn't very far away at this moment."

"*Certainly?*" Judith looked quickly at her husband. "Isn't that a bit of a guess?"

"It's a certainty founded on another certainty."

"What do you mean by that?"

"Simply this, my dear. You and I spent some time gazing at Vermeer's Aquarium only this afternoon."

5

"You and Lady Appleby *saw* the Aquarium?" The Duke of Horton had jumped to his feet. His agitation was so great that he unconsciously helped himself to another cigar. "But you must *know* the Aquarium."

Appleby provided matches. "Of course we know it very well. Only, when we saw it, it wasn't called the Aquarium, and it didn't look like the Aquarium either. It was called, if I remember rightly, The Fifth and Sixth Days of Creation. Not that it looked like *that*, any more than it looked like a lot of small fish in a tank. It might just as well have been called Battle of the Bacteria, or Project for a New Satellite Town. But that's a point of only the most superficial interest." Appleby turned to his wife. "Do you know, earlier this evening I was worried by a notion that Cadover, quite unwittingly, had said something extremely illuminating about the whole affair? Now I remember what it was. He said about Limbert's death that suicide was the superficial picture, and that there might be something quite different beneath the surface. It was a quite brilliant sally by his unconscious mind."

"It didn't get me back my picture." The Duke was suddenly sunk in gloom. "And I wish I knew what you were talking about."

"And I could have bought it. I was offered it." Appleby allowed himself for the moment to be more charmed by the fantasy of the thing than was altogether considerate to his bewildered guest. "There was Judith's little man Braunkopf expending all his arts in order to persuade me to buy Vermeer's Aquarium for something round about two hundred guineas. Either to hang in this drawing-room as a background for Judith's latest fawn, or to present to the Tate."

"Present the Aquarium to the *Tate*?" Words almost failed the Duke.

"Braunkopf assured me that by doing so I should earn the particular approbation of the royal family. He was still doing his best to close the deal when we turned round and saw that the Aquarium had been stolen."

"Stolen? But of course it had been stolen!"

"Stolen all over again, sir. Or perhaps one should say re-stolen."

"I must say, my dear chap, that you seem in dashed good spirits about this. . . . Thank you, m'dear." The Duke acknowledged Judith's politic pouring out of a further supply of brandy. "I hope there's something in it to be pleased about."

"I think there is." Appleby spoke soberly again. "You see, thanks to the link provided by Limbert's possession of the Stubbs, we already know much more about the fortunes of the Vermeer than we could rea-

82

sonably have hoped for at this stage. It has been disguised as another picture. That would be technically possible, Judith?"

"Certainly. It would be the best thing to do. Any competent painter would know how to put down a plain ground, which would protect the surface absolutely, and then paint anything that took his fancy. If the picture was then to be smuggled out of the country, a skin of fresh canvas would be put on the back, and the stretcher faked up a bit where necessary. The fraud would then defy all but the most expert examination. And it wouldn't be likely to get that. Americans are constantly buying modern paintings and carting them out of Europe."

Appleby looked up suddenly. "There's more to it than that. In fact, there's a point of some significance there. But it will keep for the moment. We have to get back to thinking about Limbert. There he was—apparently with the Duke's Stubbs displayed on his wall, and the Duke's Vermeer in process of being put into hiding on his easel. And then somebody kills him. Well, there were high stakes involved."

"That's all very well. But whoever killed Limbert failed to get away with either the Vermeer or the Stubbs."

"The affair must be admitted to have its puzzling features."

"It doesn't seem to me to have anything else." The Duke's tone was both exasperated and plaintive. "If one of you could possibly explain——"

"Let me try." And while Judith launched out upon an account of the death of Gavin Limbert and its sequel at the Da Vinci, her husband filled a pipe and

83

abstracted his mind. The whole affair badly needed ordering.

The most plausible hypothesis was simple enough. Young Gavin Limbert had been at once a thorough-going and a foolhardy criminal. He had been sufficiently thorough-going to become a party to a skilled professional theft—one that had involved, among other things, the forging of a letter from an Italian aristocrat, the transmission of a valuable and bulky piece of antique furniture from Rome to Scamnum Court, and some knowledge of the domestic habits of the Duke of Horton and his household. He had been sufficiently foolhardy to expose a minor fruit of his criminality, the Stubbs, upon the walls of a room apparently familiarly visited by all his acquaintance. To this one might add that he had been sufficiently unwary to get himself killed.

But—to take up this last point first—*why* had he been killed? The answer ought to be in terms of thieves falling out. Yet thieves when they fall out commonly remain thieves; and on this view the death of Limbert ought to have been accompanied by the disappearance of both the Scamnum Court pictures from his studio. Why had the opportunity been missed? And how was one to relate that missed opportunity to the daring *coup* brought off at the Da Vinci that afternoon?

Limbert, moreover, had been curiously dilatory. The pictures had been removed from the Scamnum gallery on the night of Sunday the 14th of October. Limbert had been killed eight days later. At that date the Vermeer, masked by a modern abstract painting, was still in his studio. Judith had just remarked that it was easy to take such paintings out of the country, since there was always a substantial traffic in them to the United States. That was true—more or less. But in this regard the situation would decidedly change as soon as it was known to the police that one of the most important privately owned paintings in England had vanished. And the substitution at Scamnum Court of the colour print for the original Aquarium had afforded the chance of a day or two's elapsing before the theft was discovered and announced. The thieves had everything to gain by rushing the picture out of the country at top speed.

And the theft had almost certainly been planned with an eye to this time factor. It explained the choice of the Vermeer from among half a dozen paintings in the Scamnum picture gallery of almost equal value. The colour print, although it would not deceive an expert eye for a moment, might pass muster with guides and visitors for some time. And of none of the other paintings, probably, would a full size colour print have been available.

But then there was the additional theft of the Stubbs. Even a person familiar with the Duke of Horton's habits in relation to the little room where it hung would be aware that its removal would increase the chance of early discovery. Why had it been taken too? Its value was very considerable—and the more so because it could be sold virtually on an open market. But it was chicken-feed compared with Vermeer's Aquarium. The best guess seemed to be that the Stubbs had been taken upon impulse: suddenly come upon, it had proved not to be resisted.

If this was a good guess, a point of some significance followed. The man who had lurked in the Spanish chest had been himself either a painter or a person knowledgeable in painting. Had it been Limbert? Suppose that it had. Suppose that Limbert had been the principal agent in the theft, and that he had then nonchalantly hung the Stubbs above his mantelpiece and proceeded to conceal the Vermeer beneath a rapidly executed composition of his own. There was nothing against this—or nothing except a mere impression of Limbert's personality—an impression which Appleby acknowledged as having come to him on very slender grounds. And it was a supposition with which a good deal fitted neatly in. For instance, one might ask oneself this question: Would Limbert be concerned to give any special character to a painting simply intended to conceal what lay beneath it? And the answer was obvious. He would make it unlike his own normal work, and thereby be the better able to disown it if there was later any question of tracing it back to him.

But here Appleby pulled himself up. The Fifth and Sixth Days of Creation—if by that plain improvisation of Hildebert Braunkopf's the composition was really to be known—was acknowledged to be in a new manner so far as Limbert was concerned. So far, so good. *But Zhitkov had claimed to have seen Limbert at work on it more than once.* Limbert had gone openly about the job, just as he had openly displayed the stolen Stubbs on his studio wall. Unless, that was to say, Zhitkov was a liar—as he very well might be.

What other factors had to be considered? There was the girl called Mary Arrow, who had been on terms at least of friendship with Limbert; and who, ten days ago, had picked up a tooth-brush and vanished. There was Zhitkov himself, who had been the agent in the discovery of Limbert's body, and who had crept up the fire-escape to spy upon events in Mary Arrow's room. There was Boxer, the other regular inhabitant of the house in Gas Street, together with his massive model, Grace Brooks. There was the unknown man with whom Limbert, on the day of his death, had been involved in a row. There was the topography of the house, and the odd fact of its virtual isolation during the raid upon the Thomas Carlyle. Last of all, there was the abstracting of the disguised Aquarium from the Da Vinci that afternoon. And this, in a sense, brought the inquiry round full circle, since it reintroduced what was surely the crucial question of all: Why were the two stolen paintings left undisturbed in Limbert's studio upon the occasion of Limbert's death?

One very simple answer was possible. Limbert really had committed suicide. Caught up in a criminal enterprise alien to his character, and realising its folly, he had taken a quick way out. This, it appeared, was not inconsistent with whatever medical evidence there was. And it would explain the subsequent history of the Aquarium. As soon as Limbert's body was discovered, his studio had become inaccessible to his confederates. They had been obliged to bide their time, and now they had repossessed themselves of their booty by raiding the Da Vinci. Moreover the disappearance of Mary Arrow could be plausibly explained within this framework of supposition. Aware in some way of what had happened—perhaps having been, through her association with Limbert, directly implicated—she had been constrained to take to panic flight. In this reading of the matter, the tooth-brush could be viewed as a demoralised young woman's last grab at self-respect.

But outside all this there remained one obstinate fact. The dead man's studio had been ransacked—and ransacked by somebody unconcerned to carry off the stolen pictures. The treatment of Limbert's books, moreover, was significant; it suggested a hunt for something far from bulky. What was involved might be some species of compromising document. Limbert's killing himself might have made the finding of this urgent. Perhaps it had been the missing woman who was concerned. Her flight might have been a consequence of failure to discover something that she considered vital to her safety or her reputation.

Appleby realised that in all this there was too much of mere supposition. From the puzzle before him too many pieces were still missing. Until they turned up—until he was possessed of a little more simple factual information—nothing much could be done. Having acknowledged this to himself, Appleby emerged from his abstraction and took notice of the world around him. As he did so, Judith looked up from her colloquy with the Duke. "John," she said, "isn't that the front-door bell?"

Appleby nodded. "I'm expecting a call." And he added drily: "A friend of yours, my dear, who will be delighted to meet our guest."

Mr Hildebert Braunkopf or Brown, although evidently not altogether at his nervous ease, advanced into Lady Appleby's drawing-room in a highly professional manner. "Peautiful!" he exclaimed on the threshold. He raised both hands before him, rather like a traveller in the age of sensibility when suddenly confronted with the prospect of the Alps. "A peautiful residence and a most puffik peautiful room. But jus *there*"—and Braunkopf interrupted the bowing and bobbing process habitual to him in order to shoot out a fat white finger dramatically at a vacant stretch of wall—"jus there, Lady Abbleby, is one voonderble obbortunity to hang some puttikler fine *chef-d'œuvre* yunker art of to-day I find you very choice cheap."

Appleby nodded. "What we want, Mr Brown, is acid greens and strong diagonals. But that must wait. Let me introduce you to the Duke of Horton. Mr Hildebert Brown."

"Goot Lort!" Braunkopf stood up to this moment well. His eyebrows, indeed, arched themselves abruptly— but his words were apparently designed as an appropriate and respectful appellative rather than as an expression of surprise. "Goot Lort, how you do— yes?"

"The Duke has come up to town in order to look about for some pictures." Appleby was unable to resist this somewhat disingenuous, if literally true, statement.

Braunkopf threw up his hands again, this time in vast dismay. "And the goot lort had no cart my most important liddle private view to-day attended lonk list of other nobilities! This choking omittance due my princible secretaries absent on continent arranging large exhibitions modern masters."

"The Duke's pictures at Scamnum Court are mostly old masters, not modern ones."

Braunkopf bobbed. "I know very well that monster national treasure-house genuine old masters."

"Nothing national about it." The Duke, touched upon a point of strong conviction, spoke abruptly. "Or nothing except the butter and the flour in the kitchens. And they're poor stuff."

89

"I know very well that puttikler perfek room all hunk extra large genuine Van Dyke." Braunkopf, unaware that this confounding of the splendours of Scamnum Court with the modest pretensions of Wilton House must appear highly absurd to his new acquaintance, beamed happily on the Duke. "You in residings at Claridge's—yes?"

"Eh? Oh, I see. I generally put up at Brown's."

"I send there, time you name tomorrow, my big Daimler." Braunkopf frowned, as if reproaching himself for this altogether inadequate flight of fancy. "I send one my three four new big Daimler cars bring you to my historical important exhibition entire surviving work Gavin Limbert."

"I'm afraid I shan't be able to manage it, Mr—um—Brown. I go back to Scamnum to-night."

Braunkopf did not allow himself to be cast down by this. Indeed, his predatory eye brightened. "Then better I send to Scamnum this whole extravagant important collection of Limberts for liddle private view. The Da Vinci is always doing pig affairs that sort. I got three five pig pantechnicons perpechal carrying selek private views gentlemen's and nobles' bottoms."

"Bottoms?" The Duke was rather dazed.

"The Limbert private view arrive Scamnum, your stately bottom, middle nex week. No deposit, and carriage and insurance paid. You keep the whole lot as lonk you like. Settlement at your conveniences later."

"It's a pity you can't include Limbert's last work, Mr Brown." Appleby at this point thought it desirable to come to the rescue of the Duke. "It's a pity The Fifth and Sixth Days of Creation has vanished."

Braunkopf was dismayed. "Your police not yet

90

found that, Sir John? When you runk up asking me call on puttikler important matter, I thought you found my picture."

"Well, I haven't. And it's not your picture. It's the Duke's picture. And it isn't in any substantial sense a Limbert at all." Appleby was watching Braunkopf narrowly. "Didn't you know?"

It looked as if Braunkopf had not known. His bewilderment appeared genuine. And there was, of course, very little reason to suppose that it would be otherwise. "The Duke's picture?" he cried.

"Yes. From what you are pleased to call his bottom—his country seat. Limbert's picture is no more than a skin of paint over another picture, stolen from Scamnum Court. In fact, Mr Brown, what you were trying to sell me this afternoon was Vermeer's Aquarium."

"Jan Vermeer of Delft!"

"Yes—and pretty well what you would call his *chef-d'œuvre*. A number of factors make it virtually certain that Limbert painted that abstract picture on top of it in order to smuggle it out of the country. That, of course, is why the thing was stolen from your gallery this afternoon. Gavin Limbert was no doubt an interesting young painter, and the mystery surrounding his death has made your show something of a sensation. But nobody would go to the trouble of *stealing* a Limbert. Would they now, Mr Brown?"

Astonishment for the moment brought Braunkopf to terms with simple veracity. He nodded his head in mute agreement. "A puffik genuine high-class Vermeer of Delft!" he presently murmured. Then he turned to the Duke. "But Sir John will recover it. And I shall find you a purchaser, goot lort, at two three

91

hundred thousand dollars." Braunkopf was himself again. "Commission only five per cent. And I give you liddle discount entire works yunk genius Gavin Limbert."

"It's Limbert we have to talk about." Appleby motioned Braunkopf to a chair, at the same time treating him to a grimly professional glance. "This stolen picture, which is certainly of very great value, has been in your possession; and there are one or two questions which I must ask you to answer now. First, there is your association with Limbert. Am I to understand that you knew him personally?"

"Knew Limbert personally?" Braunkopf licked his lips. He had quite suddenly become a very shifty and defensive person. "You mean, Sir John, was he a goot freunt of mine?"

"You know what I mean very well." Appleby spoke with brusque impatience. "I want to know all about your dealings with him. He brought you pictures to sell?"

"To try to sell. It is very hard to sell the works of the yunker painters. Even the Da Vinci finds it hard. And with Limbert and his whole group it has been very hard."

"Limbert belonged to a group—he had associates? That's just the sort of thing I want to know, Mr Brown. I see that you are going to assist us greatly." Appleby was urbane again. "And, as a group, they were unrecognised, as far as a market went?"

Braunkopf nodded. "Until there was this pig strike of luck, Sir John——"

"A big stroke of luck?"

"Until Limbert died with such pig sensations"— Braunkopf was recovering tone—"nothing could be done. I showed paintings and carvings by Limbert and his freunts regularly in the Da Vinci. But nobodies ever wanted to buy them—or nobodies who could pay."

"Would you say that the group felt any sense of grievance over that? Did they feel that they were up against a hard world, and must grab what they could from it?"

"But of course." The question clearly puzzled Braunkopf. "Everybodies feels that. Life is crab. Life is crab what you can when you can—no? But I forget. Life too is art. And peauty." At this last reflection Braunkopf, with fine presence of mind, remembered to cast an admiring eye upon both Lady Appleby and her drawing-room.

"Were Limbert and his friends a bit wild? Did they talk about taking action against society—that sort of thing? For instance"—Appleby glanced at the Duke—"did they denounce wealthy people who prided themselves on collections of old masters but never thought of doing anything for artists who still had the job of keeping themselves alive?"

"Poxer talkes like that."

"Poxer? You mean Boxer, the painter who has a studio in the same house as Limbert's in Gas Street?"

"That is correk, Sir John. Poxer."

"And Limbert himself?"

Braunkopf shook his head. "Limbert never talked about the wronks of artists. You must reklekt, Sir Johnt, his fambly support him handsome. Limbert crabbed, but when he crabbed he paid. Like I remember once—" Suddenly Braunkopf stopped. "Like I remember nothink."

"Come, come, Mr Brown. I can see that you have recalled something important."

"A liddle mistakings, Sir John. Now I tell you more most importantest informings on Limbert's other freunts."

"We'll come to that. But it's not what I want at the moment." Appleby was inexorable. "Limbert took what he wanted without ceremony, but what he took he paid for. You were saying something like that, and you were going on to speak of an actual instance. It sounds like linking up with something else about Limbert—something I have heard about the last day of his life. So I must have it. Speak up."

But Braunkopf was now engaged in odd contortions, conventionally to be described as struggling for breath. Under the stress of some obscure emotion, moreover, the complexion of the Da Vinci's proprietor had become tinged with an appropriately Leonardo-like shade of green. Suddenly—and even more surprisingly—he gave vent to a dismal howl. And this presently modulated into a semi-articulate wail. "The Jan Vermeer of Delft, Sir John, Lady Abbleby, my goot lort. I could have had it . . . in old Moe's . . . for fifteen shillinks down."

Judith—whose protégé, after all, Braunkopf was—charitably provided brandy. But at the same time she addressed him with some sternness. "Old Moe, Mr Brown? Do you mean old Moe Steptoe?"

"Yes, Lady Abbleby. It is not that I do businesses with Moe. All the business connectings of the Da Vinci are most puttikler respekful and high-class. It was just that I met Limbert looking in Moe's window."

Appleby turned to his wife. "Who on earth is old Moe Steptoe?"

"A shocking old rascal with a junk shop in Chelsea. I'd be surprised if your people at Scotland Yard didn't prove to have a line on him. He's said to be quite a power in the inferior regions of the shady picture business."

"Which is why our respectable friend here would do no more than take a peep at his window." Appleby turned to Braunkopf. "Would you agree with my wife that the police are probably interested in this Moe Steptoe?"

"That was the point, Sir John. The polices were there—behind Limbert and me."

"I see. And that, I suppose, was very unnerving for you all."

"It was unnervinks for old Moe. He was in a panic. And now I think I see that was why Limbert got the pictures."

"Got the pictures? I think we'd better have a more coherent account of this. To begin with, when did it happen?"

Braunkopf considered. "It was a Monday afternoon. Not last Monday, but the Monday before."

"In fact, Monday the 15th of October. And Limbert was looking at this man Steptoe's window. And you, Mr Brown, came up with him and passed the time of day. Then you both went into the shop together. Is that right?"

"Correk, Sir John. Limbert asked me to pack him up."

"To pack him up?"

"To pack him up in the pargaining, if he saw what he wanted."

95

"And what did he want?"

Braunkopf looked surprised. "Why, Sir John, he wanted canvases, of course."

"You mean that this fellow Steptoe, as well as having a junk shop, sells artists' materials—that he is, in fact, a colourman, and so forth?"

"Nothinks of the kint, Sir John. The yunker painters often buy olt junk-shop oil-paintings to paint on. They are less——"

"What an idiot I've been!" Appleby, staring in fascination at Braunkopf, reached for the brandy bottle himself. "A new, properly primed canvas is very expensive nowadays, so Limbert was looking for a few old pictures to serve instead. And you were helping him. And, for some reason, there were policemen in the offing. That's clear enough. Now go on."

"There was nobodies in the shop, and so we poked about. Limbert saw nothink that was any goot to him. He was sometimes a very impatient yunk man. He shouted. And it was just as he shouted, Sir John, that the two plain-clothes polices came into the shop behind us. I recognised them at once."

"Did you indeed, Mr Brown. That is most interesting."

"I had been of assistings to them before." Braunkopf made this explanation with some dignity. "One was Inspector Cow——"

"Gow—and the other would be Fox. They chase up certain kinds of stolen goods, and works of art among others. Go on, Mr Brown."

"Behind the shop there is a shed, where old Moe works. When Limbert got no replyings to that shout, he gave the door one pig kick and walked in. Moe

96

was there. He turned round with a great chump. He was very furry."

"Steptoe turned with a jump and was in a great fury. Why?"

"He was busy with his privates."

"What we call his private affairs, Mr Brown. And what were they, at that moment?"

"He was standing before a pig canvas with a fresh white ground. As soon as Limbert saw that canvas, Sir John, he said: 'Moe, I'll take that one. It might do for what I have in mind.'"

"Was there anything unusual about this?"

"Nothink, Sir John—nothink at all. Moe can put down a fresh ground on an old canvas, and often passes the time that way. It adds a few shillinks to the price."

"I see. Well?"

"'Not for sale,' Moe says—and it is then I see he is in a panic. And at that moment, before you could vink an eyelash, in comes Cow."

"And Fox?"

"In come both these plain-clothes polices. Moe knows them very well. He palls."

Appleby chuckled. "The same can't be said of your story. Steptoe turns pale. Proceed."

"For a minute the polices jus stand, looking crim. And Limbert says: 'Moe, you olt rascal, why shouldn't it be for sale? I'll give fifteen bob, and don't talk none-senses.' Moe says nothing for a pit. His chaw has dropped, and his eyes are pupping—pupping out of his head with panic. Limbert picks up the canvas— for the ground has some new quick-drying stuff—and pulls out fifteen shillinks. Then his eye falls on a small painting propped against a table-leg. 'What's this?' he says—and takes a lonk look at it. 'Nice junk-shop

97

school of Stubbs, eh?' 'You put that down,' Moe says. 'It's exposed for sale,' Limbert says. 'And five bob's the price of a nice junk-shop school of Stubbs.' 'Nothink of the sort,' Moe cries. 'What,' says Limbert; 'you're not claiming it as a real Stubbs, are you?' Moe gives a kind of wriggle. The two polices are still standing there, waiting to ask him questions about some burglarisings. Moe is embraced. Sir John, Lady Abbleby, goot lort—I think I never seen a man so embraced before."

Appleby nodded. "And this embarrassment is so powerful that Steptoe gives way?"

"Jus that. 'Of course it's not a real Stubbs,' he says— and his voice has a kind of crack in it. 'Who'd find a real Stubbs in a shop like mine?' 'Then here's your five bob,' Limbert says; and he pulls out a pount note and puts the silver back in his pocket. 'So long, Moe. Mustn't keep your customers waiting.' And out we go with both the little oil and the pig canvas. And Limbert isn't satisfied with the canvas after all. 'I'll never paint anythink on a bloody think that shape,' he says. 'Brown, you can have it for the fifteen bob I gave olt Moe.' But of course, Sir John, I had no uses for a blank canvas. A blank canvas is no more attractings than a blank wall. No rooms wealthy cultivated patrons of peauty should have blank walls, Lady Abbleby—no?"

The Duke of Horton, who had listened with profound, if somewhat bewildered attention to the broken narrative of the proprietor of the Da Vinci Gallery, finished his brandy and stood up. "Appleby, my dear fellow, hadn't we better find this atrocious scoundrel Steptoe at once?"

"He must certainly be dropped on to-night. But I think you had better leave it to the police. I assure you we'll waste no time. Steptoe may have the Aquarium back in his possession now."

"Safe and sound? I don't like this talk of the villain putting down a ground. I don't understand it. Does it mean that this painter Limbert could actually paint a picture of his own on it, without knowing what was underneath?"

"I think it does." It was Judith who answered. "All he would know was that he had an old seventeenth or eighteenth century canvas to work on. And that's common enough. Some paintings would need several levelling coats before a new ground was put down— either that, or a lot of the old picture-surface removed with soda. But not a Vermeer. Almost nothing would show through. Certainly not enough to give him any hint of the underlying composition."

"So this fellow Limbert may have been a perfectly innocent party to the whole affair?"

"We can't be sure of that." It was now Appleby who spoke. "Limbert certainly knew he'd got a genuine Stubbs out of Steptoe. And although he had no means of tracing its owner, he must have had a strong suspicion that Steptoe had come by it wrongfully. There could be no other explanation of Steptoe's relinquishing it as he did rather than risk attracting the attention of Gow and Fox. And that should have set him thinking about the big canvas. But he mayn't have thought about it much. Indeed, if the account given me by Grace Brooks of Limbert's encounter with a stranger on his own staircase was at all accurate, that stranger can only have been Steptoe, who had run Limbert to earth and was trying to get back the pictures. If Limbert had been unsuspecting about the canvas up till then, or not disposed to bother, it seems likely that his being pestered by Steptoe put him in a different mind. And within a few hours of that he was dead."

6

Looking back upon the events of that night, Appleby was to feel that he had gone rather light-heartedly to work at the task of recovering the Scamnum Court Vermeer. And that, he admitted, was wrong. For the Aquarium was not only extremely valuable; it was extremely beautiful as well. All the resources of Scotland Yard ought to have been organised to ensure its safe recovery. Nevertheless, Appleby attacked the business in terms of a one-man show. Perhaps he was influenced by what he had heard about the fiasco of the large-scale operation at the Thomas Carlyle. More probably, it was simply a matter of self-confidence born of a long and successful career in controlling crime. Be this as it may, Appleby walked out of his own house, took a bus to Sloane Square, and presently found himself outside the junk shop of old Moe Steptoe. The place was in darkness. But this, of course, was to be expected. The time was close on ten o'clock.

Appleby walked past without pausing. The mean street was poorly lit. He could just distinguish a torn blind drawn partly down over an accumulation of broken and dusty lumber. Above, an almost illegible board appeared to intimate that Mr Steptoe was a dealer in curios and antiques. Appleby went round the block without meeting more than a stray cat; and this time he paused in Steptoe's doorway to light his pipe. A notice hung askew behind the glass, announcing that the establishment was closed. And a more substantial view of its contents made it possible to wonder why it should ever open, so extremely improbable did it appear that any of the goods displayed should again become actual articles of commerce. There was a cardboard box full of hacked and blackened golf balls, and beside this was a tennis-racket of nineteenth-century pattern, devoid of strings. There were saucepans with holes and jugs without handles; a pile of rotting canvas probably held itself out as being a carpet or rug; a shallow glass-topped box displayed a gruesome little cemetery of moths and butterflies mostly crumbled to dust. The only work of fine art on view was an oleographic reproduction of the Laughing Cavalier with a triangular tear over the nose. Presumably the recesses of the place, quite invisible to Appleby in the near darkness, would contain deposit upon deposit of the same dismal rubbish.

Appleby crossed the narrow street. It was probable that Steptoe lived either above his place of business or at the back. Here and there along the row of buildings there were lights in upper rooms, but over the junk shop there was only darkness. Appleby again walked to the end of the block, this time counting his paces. There was a narrow and unlighted lane at the back; he paced up this until he knew that he was at the rear of Steptoe's premises. Braunkopf had spoken of a shed in which Steptoe worked. Producing and cautiously using a torch, Appleby decided that he could just see the sloping roof of this structure at the end of a small yard lying behind an eight-foot brick wall. As with the other buildings down the lane, there was access to the yard through double gates. There would just be room, probably, to back in a van for the purpose of delivering or removing goods. Appleby gave a shove, and concluded that this barrier was bolted on the inside. He poked about the lane, found an abandoned ash-bin, up-ended it, scrambled to the top of the wall, and dropped down on the other side.

He paused, pleased at the success of this lawless proceeding. There was still nothing but darkness before and around him. Again he flashed on his torch. The shed occupied about half the yard; it had a door giving on the yard; but there must also be access to it direct from the shop, the back of which formed its farther wall. Appleby examined it carefully, but without much hope of getting in. The door of the shed was certainly locked and bolted; the window was secured by shutters and a substantial padlock. He moved round the shed and found the back entrance to the main business premises. This too was locked. Without hesitation, Appleby knocked—very loudly. He waited no more than ten seconds and then knocked again. The knock on the door in the dark. It was almost necessary to believe, he thought, that cave-men had doors, so obscure and primitive is the response stirred by that summons. There was nothing but silence, a murmur of distant traffic, the melancholy hoot of a single siren from some craft down the river. He

103

knocked a third time. A light went on in Steptoe's shop.

"Who's that?" A surly voice spoke from the other side of the door.

"Plain-clothes police."

"How am I to know that? You're probably thieves. Go away."

"Open the door on the chain, and take my warrant card."

"I'll do nothing of the sort. I've valuable property here—very valuable indeed—and you may be armed. It's most unreasonable. If you were in uniform it would be another matter."

"Very well, Mr Steptoe. There's something to be said for that. I'll have a uniformed man front and back within five minutes. And I'll be back myself with a search-warrant in half-an-hour."

"A search-warrant? I don't believe you're the police at all." Steptoe's voice was contemptuous, but also discernibly alarmed. "No policeman would talk such rubbish. Where do you expect to get a search-warrant at this time of night?"

"I happen to be an Assistant Commissioner of Police. There won't be any difficulty."

There was a moment's silence. Steptoe was taking stock of the situation. "Very well," he said. "I'll believe you." A bolt went back with a click. "But I warn you that I'm armed."

"Armed, Mr Steptoe? With something you have a licence for?"

"I didn't mean that." There was a sound of footsteps hastily retreating and presently advancing again. Another bolt went back, and then a key turned. The door swung open. Appleby found himself looking at the

104

point of a rusty sabre, which Steptoe had clearly produced from stock. "Come in, then." Steptoe took a pace backwards, peered sharply at Appleby, and at once thrust his weapon into a battered umbrella stand. "Good evening, sir. I'm sorry to have been a bit doubtful. But I have to be very careful."

Appleby understood that he had been recognised. "No doubt, Mr Steptoe—particularly with the very valuable property you keep here."

"That was only in a manner of speaking, sir." Steptoe looked alarmed. "One has to keep up public confidence with remarks of that sort. But the truth is that business is very poor at present—very poor, indeed. I was remarking on it to my friend Inspector Gow only the other day, sir. It's having strict standards. Those that ask no questions about where second-hand goods come from get the trade every time. I'm afraid dishonesty is rife, sir—rife in the whole community, in spite of the wonderful efforts of the police. And probity has always been the motto of this firm. Or to be exact, sir, probity and service. But it makes life very hard."

"I understand, Mr Steptoe, that you are well known to certain branches of the police—as a martyr to high standards of business rectitude, no doubt."

"It's kind of you to say so, sir—very kind indeed." Steptoe treated his visitor to an uncertain leer. Old Moe was not particularly old—nor indeed particularly anything else. His type was that conventionally described as nondescript. Unless—as seemed improbable—it was the inflexible honesty to which he laid claim, he was devoid of any outstanding characteristic whatever. Now he was moving backwards through the rear portion of his establishment. This mode of progress might have been intended as a mark of respect to an Assistant Commissioner, or as a residual caution in face of the possibility of physical assault—or it was perhaps adopted merely because the place was so crammed with every sort of hideous, useless, maimed and degraded object that turning round was an operation of some difficulty. "Perhaps, sir, you would care to step upstairs to the office? We can have a comfortable talk there. And if there is any information I can give you——"

"I'm hoping to get more than information out of you, Mr Steptoe. Lead the way."

The staircase was narrow, rickety, and for the greater part appropriated to the purpose of a set of book-shelves. Appleby's glance as he climbed was engaged by successive levels—in every sense—of literary activity. And here alone was there some evidence of a lurking instinct for order on the part of the proprietor—made manifest, however, upon somewhat uncertain principles. *King Lear* had been set beside *Queen Victoria and her People* and *The Republic of Plato*. A battered *Divine Comedy* was companioned by *A Thousand Miles of Miracles in China*, and next to this was *Twenty Thousand Leagues under the Sea*. *Little Women* had been paired with *Great Expectations; In Tune with the Infinite* with *The Theory of Harmony*; and *Petrol Engines* with *Filled with the Spirit*. Appleby had not done chuckling at this when he was ushered into what Steptoe chose to call his office.

The room had all the appearance of being bedroom and kitchen too—and bathroom whenever anything in the nature of ablution occurred to its owner. A littered desk, however, together with an ancient typewriter, a telephone and a filing-cabinet, gave a sufficient suggestion of business activity. Old Moe, by the simple expedient of removing a frying-pan from one end of a battered horse-hair sofa, accommodated his guest with a seat. "And now, sir, how can I help you? Inspector Gow will have told you that I am always ready to rally to the side of law and order—very ready, indeed. And if there is any information—" Steptoe broke off short, and slapped his forehead dramatically with his fingers. "But first, sir, do you mind if I make a telephone-call? A purely family matter. Your arrival put it quite out of my head. And it's urgent, sir—a matter of illness."

"Go ahead, Mr Steptoe."

Steptoe dialled a number. "Moe here," he said. "I'm anxious about Auntie Aggie . . . taken poorly again? Oh dear!" Steptoe's voice expressed extreme distress and concern. "It can be dangerous when they're took that way—very dangerous indeed. You must have the doctor . . . I said you must have the doctor. See if he can arrange to get her away quick. . . . Poor old soul—is that so? Ted would help— and perhaps Alfie. . . . Sad—very sad. If only something would lie on what's left of her stummik."

And Steptoe put down the receiver. "Family responsibilities, sir. They weigh on me heavily, I'm bound to confess. Those sort of ties are not acknowledged of—not as they used to be. It makes it harder on the conscientious members. And as you'll have gathered, I'm very fond of old Auntie Aggie."

"No doubt, Mr Steptoe." The somewhat primitive performance to which he had just been treated amused Appleby a good deal. Perhaps it had been rash to let Steptoe send out this absurd call. But it had settled any doubts that it was possible to feel about the man's involvement in the theft of the Vermeer. Auntie Aggie and the Aquarium were certainly one—and in danger and to be got away quick. What remained obscure was the painting's present whereabouts. Was it here on the premises, and would Ted, Alfie and the doctor presently arrive to rescue it? Or were they merely being enjoined to get it away from somewhere else? Meanwhile Appleby nodded genially to old Moe. "I hope," he said, "that your aunt will soon be quite her old self again. She probably needs a change of air."

Steptoe received this gratefully. "Thank you, sir. It's a great pleasure to have your expression of interest." His glance went furtively to a clock ticking on the mantelpiece. "And now I'm at leisure—quite at leisure, sir—for our little talk."

But leisure, it seemed to Appleby, was just what wouldn't do. The telephone-call had certainly got something moving—and that was all to the good. The first necessity was to bring out into the open as much as possible of the organisation concerned in the theft of the Vermeer. Steptoe himself was a smooth rascal, but it seemed very unlikely that he was a prime mover in the affair. He had cunning, it was true. But more than cunning had been involved. Somewhere at work there had been an educated—or at least informed—brain. Somebody had been in a position to find out quite a lot about the domestic routine of Scamnum Court, to write a colourable letter ostensibly from a cultivated Italian, to arrange for the despatch of a valuable piece of furniture from Italy to England. Steptoe's part had possibly been no more than that of receiving and disguising the stolen paintings—an activity which might well be one of his regular lines of business. And he had lamentably fallen down on his job. The combination of Gow, Fox and a masterful Gavin Limbert had been too much for him, and the booty had been snatched from his grasp. It was certainly his own individual effort to retrieve the situation that had been witnessed by Grace Brooks. The next attempt—the successful raid on the Da Vinci Gallery—had presumably been the work of the organisation as a whole. What, then, was the position at that point?

The thieves had got back the Aquarium, which was the vastly more important part of their haul. And they had got it back effectively disguised by the labours—presumably unconsciously performed—of Limbert. But that particular disguise was now of no use to them. For Limbert's was also now a stolen painting, and to be safe the Vermeer must be disguised all over again. Would this once more be entrusted to Steptoe? If so, the picture must be concealed in or around the junk shop now, and Steptoe's telephone-call had been a summoning of assistance. But if Steptoe had not again been entrusted with the picture, then the telephone-call had been simply a warning. Moe had certainly been astute enough to guess that the appearance in his back yard of a high official of Scotland Yard was not occasioned by any minor act of lawlessness. He had realised that his connection with the big theft was known.

So far, the game had gone in Appleby's favour, he had learnt a good deal that he wanted to know. But there was considerable danger that the initiative might now pass to the other side—the more so as his lonehand venture had put him momentarily out of contact with any supporting forces of his own. Leisure, he repeated, wouldn't do. He must bowl Moe out at once.

"Mr Steptoe, I suppose you are aware of the value of Vermeer's Aquarium?"

Somewhere on Steptoe's featureless face a muscle twitched. "Vermeer's Aquarium, sir? I'm afraid I don't understand you."

"I think you will presently understand me very well. His Majesty's judges, in discharging their duty to protect property, are bound to give much weight to the magnitude of a theft. To be involved in a very big theft is to risk a very long term of imprisonment." Appleby smiled pleasantly. "This has no doubt been a little on your mind."

Steptoe licked his lips with a quick movement like an adder's. "I don't know what you're talking about."

"About something quite trivial, Mr Steptoe—or trivial in comparison with another matter to which I now come. You visited Limbert's studio on Monday the 22nd of October in an endeavour to recover this picture, together with another smaller picture by George Stubbs. You failed. And the next morning Limbert was found murdered."

Steptoe stumbled to his feet. He was trembling all over. "I tell you, I know nothing about it. You're talking about things I've never heard of. You've picked on me to fasten something on, just because I've been in trouble with your people before."

"Don't be silly, Steptoe. You know we don't do that sort of thing. And there are witnesses all along the line. Gow and Fox were present when you got in a funk and let Limbert walk off with those pictures. And

110

you were seen and heard having your row with Limbert close on the time of his death. You're in a tough spot, my friend, and you'll do well to acknowledge it."

"I think you're crazy." Steptoe's glance again went furtively to the clock. "And I demand to see my lawyer. I'm going to phone him now."

"Phone away. You're rather good at phoney phoning."

"What d'you mean?"

"I mean the nonsense of your contacting Ted and Alfie and the doctor about poor Auntie Aggie. Surely you don't suppose, my good fellow, that a trick of that sort is likely to take in an experienced C.I.D. man? I've been at this sort of thing, you know, for more than twenty years. I certainly wouldn't have sat here and let you ring up your friends if I hadn't made arrangements to profit by your doing so." And Appleby shook his head indulgently. "I can see you're interested in that clock. Well, the number you called up has a police cordon round it by now." As Appleby delivered himself of the unblushing falsehood he produced and began to fill a pipe. "My notion is that you can figure in this affair much as you choose. If you are ambitious, Steptoe, you can be one of the big fish in our net. But if you think more of continuing to swim substantially undisturbed in your own shady waters—well, I think it can be arranged."

"I got to think. You must give me time to think."

"You can think afterwards. You'll have plenty of opportunity. For I'm afraid you must go to gaol. There's no getting you out of that. But perhaps just for a slip—a thoughtless little piece of receiving that you quickly repented of. You remembered, shall we

111

say, that probity has always been the motto of your firm. And so you hastened to tell the whole story to the police. And you did your best to get the poor Duke of Horton's picture back to him in quick time."

And Appleby struck a match. The life of a policeman, he was reflecting, is obstinately unbeautiful. Fortunately, it is frequently hazardous as well, which a little bolsters up one's self-respect. His own life looked like being rather hazardous during the next half-hour.

"Very well." Steptoe had sat down again. "I've been a fool. There are temptations, sir—great temptations—in my way of business."

"We'll leave that to your counsel, shall we? Your moral struggles may be relevant in court. But I'm concerned with the Vermeer. Where is it now?" Appleby rapped this out in a sharper tone than he had used hitherto.

"Not here, sir. I said I wouldn't have it in the place again. I was washing my hands of the whole thing— I was indeed, sir."

"Do you call that telephone message washing your hands of the whole thing?"

"I only want them to go away, picture and all, and leave me alone. What was I going to make out of it anyway? Fifty quid—fifty bleeding quid, sir, believe me. Downright unfair, it was."

"I certainly agree with you." Appleby's ears were now straining for more than Steptoe's mutterings. "But you haven't told me where they have the Vermeer now. Out with it."

"Not far off—not at all far off, sir." Steptoe was as urgent with this as if it constituted an extenuating circumstance in itself. "Only a couple of streets away.

112

Where they are lodging, sir—them as I was calling up. Your people will have got them by now, I dare say." Steptoe gave Appleby a swift glance of some sharpness. "In fact you might say it's all over, bar the unpleasantness for us that have been fairly caught. So if you'd care to take down a statement——"

"Just hand me that telephone."

"Certainly, sir." Steptoe pushed the instrument across his desk. It appeared to stick half-way and Steptoe stooped down and gave a tug. "It's the cord, sir—caught round the leg . . . there you are."

Appleby picked up the receiver and knew in an instant that it was dead. Steptoe had wrenched away a connection. The man was glaring at him now, apprehensive but defiant. And in the same moment Appleby heard sounds below them, either in the shop or out in the yard. "You are an obstinately silly fellow," he said calmly. "Nothing can save you and your friends, and you know it. You'll only make matters worse by trying to put up a show."

"You stay where you are, mister." With a good deal of dexterity, Steptoe had produced an automatic pistol and was pointing it at Appleby's chest. He appeared to take satisfaction in having achieved this less respectful form of address. "Make a move, and it isn't us will be done for."

Appleby got to his feet. "Put that down, man. You're not the hero of a gangster film, you know. You're a thoroughly scared small crook."

The weapon wavered in Steptoe's hand—and then steadied again. A wisp of hair, damp with sweat, had fallen over his forehead, and his mouth was oddly twisted, as if he had suddenly suffered a stroke. The man was dangerous, after all. But the chances were that he would hesitate; that fear would make him hang a fatal fraction of a second on the trigger. Appleby leant forward and struck the weapon upwards. It spat fire as the muzzle rose. Between the report and the clattering of the gun to the floor the office disappeared into darkness. Appleby found himself wondering whether he had been grazed and stunned. Then the truth of the situation came to him. Pure chance had guided the bullet to the only electric light-bulb in the room.

Somewhere in the darkness Steptoe panted like a man exhausted by physical labour. Downstairs there were voices raised in urgent consultation, and from the yard came the sound of a motor engine starting into life. Time was precious. Appleby felt in a pocket for his torch. As his fingers closed on it something queer closed about his own legs. He drew out his hand again to protect himself and realised that Steptoe's panting was now hard up against him. He was a craven creature and his knees must literally have failed to support him after he had tried to fire the gun. At the same time he was desperate and dogged; he wasn't supplicating for mercy; he was attempting a sort of static Rugger tackle that would prevent his opponent from leaving the room. Appleby punched into the darkness and the blow landed on something soft, elicited an ugly grunt. But the grip had not relaxed, and now Appleby felt a sudden sharp pain in his calf. There could be only one explanation; the feeble ruffian, bemused and frantic, was using his teeth. Something peculiarly revolting attached to the idea of being bitten by old Moe. Feeling downwards, Appleby got his hands round the man's neck, and swung his head about until it came up against some-

114

thing solid. Perhaps it was the leg of a table or a corner of the desk. Appleby swung Steptoe's head away and brought it back against this useful object with a crack.

It was another unbeautiful part of the evening's work. But at least it was effective; Steptoe in the darkness was now no more of an impediment than any other inert object in the room. Appleby got out his torch and in a moment had it focussed on the door. But there were no footsteps on the stairs, and there was now no sound from the shop. Ted, Alfie and the doctor—if it was indeed they who had come in response to old Moe's telephone call—were showing no disposition to rush to their confederate's help. Probably, Appleby thought grimly, they had a much more important operation on hand. The Vermeer really had been entrusted a second time to Steptoe. And it was being carried away now.

But even as his hand fell on the door-knob Appleby turned back. In the heart of London one can seldom fail of being within hail of law-abiding fellow citizens, if not of the actual uniformed forces of the law. Nevertheless the shop below, and the little yard lying behind it, could provide one with an ugly five minutes at the hands of desperate men. Appleby flashed his torch across the floor and in a moment had located old Moe's pistol. He slipped it into his pocket and dived for the stairs.

The shop was in darkness and he didn't pause to hunt for lights. Perhaps this was a mistake, for progress in any direction whatever was so pestered by the miscellaneous rubbish here passing for curios and antiques that the beam of a small torch was a very insufficient aid to movement. Appleby trod in a half-

115

empty croquet-box, and the handle of a mallet flew up and hit him viciously on the chest—much as if minded to exact vengeance for its owner's discomfiture upstairs. In recoil from this his elbow struck the ruin of a wardrobe canted drunkenly against the wall—whereupon some complicated species of transmission brought a flat-iron crashing down from a great height into an assemblage of ewers, basins and chamber-pots at the other end of the shop. But even above this racket Appleby could now hear the roar of an engine reverberating within the narrow confines of old Moe's yard.

The engine raced, choked, failed. Its din was succeeded by shouts of rage and despair. In the peculiar obstacle-race in which he was involved, Appleby now put on a spurt. If there was the semblance of a clear path to the back of the shop, he had lost it. Vaulting bodily over a chest of drawers, he landed on the lip of a hip-bath and sent it flying from beneath him with a tinny clang. To save his balance he clutched at a hat-stand. This instantly disintegrated in his grasp, and he found himself sitting on the floor amid a litter of bamboo. He got to his feet again and saw that an oblong of light had now appeared at the back of old Moe's establishment, and that in it was silhouetted the figure of a man. There were still at least two voices in angry colloquy outside; somebody was desperately plying a self-starter; the engine turned over and once more stopped. The figure in the open doorway advanced and at the same time flashed on a torch, side-stepped, and closed the door behind him. The beam from the torch rose, fell, circled, played full on Appleby, and then went out. Instinct made Appleby duck, and as he did so some unseen object hurtled

116

past above his head and landed with a crash in the recesses of the establishment. The enemy, Appleby understood, were improvising a vigorous rearguard action.

He found that he was crouching behind an upended kitchen table. From this shelter it was open to him to produce Steptoe's pistol and essay the effect of a little random shooting. This might bring in the neighbours—but on the other hand it might make them very determined to keep out. Moreover it would be dangerous, and if by any chance he killed the man lurking somewhere in front of him it would be a shocking end to what was already a deplorably irresponsible evening. Peering out with some caution, therefore, he confined himself for the moment to a little torch-play.

The beam located the doorway, swung right, and fell full upon a human face. The eyes glared, the lips were drawn back over fang-like teeth in a ferocious snarl, and the forehead was topped with a pair of handsome horns. Appleby had just convinced himself, by a considerable if instantaneous effort of intellect, of the innocuousness of this particular antique or curio, when he became aware of fresh assault. Directly in front of him something had risen mysteriously in air. His torch, catching it as it descended, revealed a monstrous pike with gaping jaws; a moment later the creature had smashed into a hundred plaster fragments at his feet. He saw that if he was to gain the yard, and to prevent the escape of whatever motor vehicle was temporarily held up in it, he must himself initiate a vigorous counter-attack. He therefore seized such ammunition as came first to hand—a pile of coarse and formidably heavy earthenware dinner-plates—rose, and boldly advanced. A small oil-stove, a coal-scuttle, a doll's perambulator and a music-stool came about his ears in quick succession. But Appleby, behind a barrage of plates intended less to cripple the enemy than to upset his aim, went forward over sofas, under tables and through a veritable jungle growth of mangles, whatnots and jardinières. Once or twice he got tightly wedged in crevasse-like formations of massive Victorian furniture. In the worst of these narrows he thought he was stuck for good; it was like some abominable Freudian dream of the trauma of birth—with the superaddition of a constant bombardment by objects themselves dream-like or nightmarish in their inexhaustible variety. He abandoned the remainder of his dinner-plates and broke through. And at the same moment his opponent rose from cover—apparently resolved upon, or resigned to, hand-to-hand encounter.

Each still had his torch, and neither was prepared to abandon it in order to grapple. For a second therefore they paused warily, with a small cleared space between them, and around them the rubble and rubbish—now doubly pashed and pounded—of old Moe's stock. The man confronting Appleby crouched, set down his torch with a quick movement, and leapt. As he did so, the silence which had fallen upon the shop was broken by a slithering sound near the ceiling. Once again, some complicated sequence of stresses had been at work—and this time to produce a delayed-action effect of the most startling sort. Upon Appleby and his adversary as they closed there was suddenly poured from above torrent upon torrent of what seemed to be gigantic hail-stones. Not Gulliver in Brobdingnag was more cruelly assaulted. Old

118

Moe—it would have been possible upon reflection to guess—had been planning a commercial operation of major importance: nothing less than that of securing a corner in children's marbles. And now the entire stock was running down through space, much after the fashion of the atoms of Democritus as Lucretius describes them in his celebrated poem. In a moment the floor beneath the struggling men had gone crazy; it was like something in a fun-fair where one pays sixpence for the sensation of being unable to keep one's feet. They fell and rolled over and over, robbed of any control over their own limbs, like objects helplessly impelled through a system of ball-bearings. And then, outside, the engine roared again—and this time settled to a confident purr. Appleby, aware of crisis, made a grab at his man, and found his arms closing on air. The atomic deluge had operated to his disadvantage. His opponent had recovered more quickly and was gone.

And by the time he reached the yard it was empty. The gates were open. From the lane he heard the rumble of a lorry and then a grinding of gears. He dashed out in time to see a covered van of considerable size disappearing into the darkness. The position looked bad, but he knew that he had a chance yet. The van was moving in the direction of a main road. However reckless the driver might be, or however skilful, he would have to slow down—even stop—if there chanced to be a stream of traffic blocking his path. Appleby ran.

The van was slackening speed for the corner. He heard the grind of gears again and saw it lurch almost to a stop; ahead, there was a constant flicker of lights from close-travelling traffic into which the van was unable to filter. He was almost up with it when it moved again, swinging left hazardously under the nose of a bus. In front of him Appleby saw a handle and grabbed. A door swung open, and simultaneously the van checked its pace. He heard brakes scream behind him. In a second he might be pinned between van and bus—and a good deal more uncomfortably than between old Moe Steptoe's wardrobes. Appleby jumped; the van jerked forward again; the door swung to behind him. Without precisely intending it, he was actually travelling with his enemies in their own conveyance.

It was an odd achievement, and Appleby wanted to laugh. But he had had enough, he reflected, of care-free amusement for one night, and his behaviour from now on had better be entirely policemanly and rational. He still had his torch, which he had slipped into his pocket when the man in the junk shop sprang at him. And he had Steptoe's pistol. He produced both, placed himself in a posture of preparedness in the swaying van, and snapped on the light.

For a moment his heart sank. It was hard not to believe that he must have made a mistake—that he had risked his neck to no better purpose than to have boarded the wrong vehicle. For what he appeared to be in presence of was an orthodox, small-scale removal. The van was, in fact, a sort of pantechnicon. And about two-thirds of it was packed in a fully professional fashion with carpets, furniture and small crates—with everything, indeed, that goes technically by the name of household effects. The remaining third, in which he found himself, was empty except for a pile of sacking and some wisps of wood-wool. From the driver of the van, and whoever might be with him in his cab, Appleby was cut off by the entire bulk of stuff being transported. Unless and until the van stopped in some isolated situation, he was now free of any threat from his antagonists.

And they *were* his antagonists. The notion that he had made some absurd mistake was one that he could put out of his head. For this—when one came to think it out—was precisely the safest way in which to make off with a valuable picture. Stuff it into the middle of a genuine removal—or of something having all the appearance of being that—and only a very pertinacious hunt would be likely to run you to earth. The conviction grew on Appleby that for the second time that day he was virtually within arm's length of Vermeer's Aquarium. In other words, the stolen picture would be back at Scamnum Court tomorrow.

A sudden apprehension assailed Appleby even as he reached this comfortable conclusion. The door through which he had leapt had swung to behind him. Had it thereby, by any chance, closed itself more securely than when he had managed to tug it open? If so, could it be opened from the inside? Was it conceivable that he had made himself a prisoner?

He swung his torch on the door. It was in two halves, vertically divided. One of the halves had bolts engaging with the roof and floor; the other had no visible fastening at all. Neither of the bolts was thrust home, yet the whole had the appearance of being firmly secured. This looked bad. Appleby, with difficulty balancing himself on the swaying floor, gave a cautious shove. Nothing happened. He thrust harder, and both sides of the door gave, so that he expected the momentum of the van to send them flying open with a crash. But nothing of the sort occurred; a gap of less than a couple of inches appeared between the two halves, making it possible to take a squint at the outer world; and at that they obstinately stuck. With growing misgiving, Appleby investigated further. By straining hard it was possible to increase this gap by something like a further inch at the bottom. But at the top nothing whatever could be done. He guessed that some lateral bar had there fallen into place, and that he was in consequence himself as firmly imprisoned as a lion or tiger in a zoo.

But at least he now had a view. The van had as yet not gone far. It was trundling up Sloane Street in the direction of Knightsbridge, and had just passed the intersection of Pont Street. Immediately behind it was a pale green Humber saloon. Appleby wondered whether, by shouting or by waving a handkerchief through the crack, he had any chance of securing the effective intervention of the driver of this vehicle. The idea, on the whole, seemed a poor one, and he paused to think again. His object must be to have the van stopped by the police, and this he had better achieve as soon as possible. Amid the traffic of central London, indeed, the job might take a lot of doing, whereas if the van moved out through the suburbs it must come to districts the quiet of which would make attention easier to secure. On the other hand, central London is the place for policemen. The theatres would be out by now, the taxis at their busiest, and plenty of constables about with an eye on the traffic. Ten to one, the van intended to swing right for Hyde Park Corner, and the chance of its being brought to a standstill there was a substantial one. Even so, it was doubtful if anything could be done by thumping and shouting. But he still had Steptoe's gun.

As the van turned into Knightsbridge Appleby brought the pistol from his pocket. His hand grasping it would certainly not go through the crack, but at least the muzzle could be made to protrude. And a pistol spitting fire from the back of a closed van was a device admirably calculated to attract police notice.

Unfortunately Appleby could not see it as being other than uncomfortably dangerous. It was not even as if one shot would do. A number would be required, if he was to make certain that the origin of the disturbance was located. And there is no method of projecting a stream of lead into a London street without causing grave hazard. Bullets discharged high in air descend when spent with lethal momentum; bullets aimed at a highway ricochet unpredictably. Appleby took his time at this problem. He had found no solution when the van successfully negotiated Hyde Park Corner without a stop and moved at an increased speed up the Ring. That meant that in the way of major hold-ups there was still Marble Arch. Appleby peered out. The green Humber was still close behind. Hard on its tail was a muffled figure on a motor bicycle, and behind that again was an old Austin Seven.

They were running past Grosvenor Gate when a new set of considerations presented themselves to Appleby. Earlier in the evening he had been in much of a hurry to secure a little quiet fun on his own, to take a dip into his less unadventurous past. Was it really necessary now to scramble out so quickly? Rescued from a closed van by a couple of coppers on point duty, he would become for a time a very sufficient figure of fun—even if the Duke of Horton thereby got back his Vermeer. There was no harm in that. But still—why not carry on? More closely scrutinized, was

123

carrying-on not, after all, the most rational course to adopt? Helpless in this van, he might exhaust the automatic pistol without in fact attracting any attention at all—or at least without securing any effective interception. On the other hand, if he stayed put until the thing had reached its destination and was opened up, he would be armed, and his position would have all the strength of complete surprise. He had successfully confronted tougher situations often enough.

And Appleby let Marble Arch go by. The van turned into the Bayswater Road. That almost certainly meant that it was seeking one of the western arteries: the Exeter road, the Bath road, or perhaps up through Uxbridge for Beaconsfield and Oxford. He peered out once more. It was raining and the street and pavements were beginning to shine beneath their lamps. The van was still heading both the green Humber and the motor bike, and behind these he could just glimpse the little Austin. Presently he had better extinguish his torch. This journey might go on into the small hours, and it was essential to conserve the battery. But first it would be a good idea to inspect the mechanism of the automatic. Appleby sat down on sacking and put this resolution into effect.

The pistol was empty. The cartridge fired in old Moe Steptoe's office had been the last in the magazine.

7

The brandy had sunk remarkably low in its bottle before the Duke of Horton was ready to depart. Dismissing the Scamnum Vermeer from his mind without the least discernible effort, he had embarked upon an extended description of the present state of his Large Blacks. Large Blacks, it appeared, were exceedingly docile, a quietness of habit attributable to their ears, which hang well forward over the eyes. The Duke's main concern was to obtain a heavy jowl, and well-developed hind-quarters with an abundance of fine hair. The subject was one which Judith Appleby judged decidedly soporific, and she found it increasingly difficult to repel from her mind a disquieting vision of gigantic negroes, with all these attributes prominently displayed, placidly grazing the fields of Scamnum Ducis. But when her guest had finally taken his leave, with Goldfish and Silverfish tucked nonchalantly under his arm, she found herself abruptly awake again. The last thing she wanted to do was to go to bed.

And John, she well knew, might be away for hours. The affair of Gavin Limbert had got a grip on him. For that matter, it had got a grip on her too. She was wondering if her knowledge of artists and their ways could somehow be exploited to produce a fresh line on the mystery, or if she could think of some likely personal contact of Limbert's, when she was disturbed by the ringing of the telephone-bell. On picking up the receiver she was greeted with what she at first took to be a terrified scream, followed by a high-pitched gabble in Chinese. A moment later she knew that she was merely listening to the excited voice of Mervyn Twist.

"Dear Lady Appleby, what a pleasure to run into you this afternoon! But have you heard the terrible news?"

"You mean the theft of that picture from the Da Vinci?"

"Yes, indeed. But of course you have. You were still in the gallery when it happened. It makes me quite ill to think of it."

"My being in the gallery when it happened?"

"No—no indeed, dear Lady Appleby . . . Judith." Twist's voice rose to yet a higher pitch, so that Judith wondered if it ever became blessedly inaudible except to the very young, like the squeaking of bats. "I am *so* upset—and positively *épuisé*. With horror. And with *uneasiness*. I feel there is something that I might have done."

"About Limbert?"

"Yes, indeed. I wish I could confide in you. Is your husband at home?"

"No. He's had to go out."

"Dear Judith, might I come round?"

"No." Judith found that she had given this uncompromising answer before thinking of any reasonably civil sequel to it. "The dog is rather upset," she said. "I suppose these things are catching. It might bite you."

"Oh, dear!" Twist gave a squeak of alarm. "Could you come out somewhere and have a drink? Could you make the Thomas Carlyle?"

"The place at the bottom of Gas Street?"

"Yes, indeed. But that's not the entrance. You go——"

"I know. Yes, I'll come. Thank you very much." Mervyn Twist, Judith thought, might really have something to tell, since he was an indefatigable hanger-round in the studios of advanced painters. Moreover the Thomas Carlyle, although not known to be actually implicated in the Limbert mystery, was, topographically at least, intriguingly peripheral to it. "I'll come right away," Judith said. "Are you a member?"

"Indeed, yes—isn't it absurd?" Twist produced a piercing self-conscious giggle. "May I come and fetch you in a taxi?"

"Thank you very much—but please don't."

"The dog?"

"Yes. He's producing an odd sort of foam at the mouth and seems *very* excited. Of course if you know about dogs, and would care to have a *look* at Tiger——?"

"That's the dog?"

"Yes. We call him that because of his being so fierce even at ordinary times. . . . But what was I saying?"

"Dear Judith, you were saying that you would hop

into a taxi and come straight along to the Thomas Carlyle. Just ask for me at the door and I'll be there in a *jiffy*." Twist giggled again at the skittish phrase. "It will be a comfort. To *tell* you. Yes, indeed."

"I'll be glad to listen." And Judith hung up, scribbled a note for John, and called a taxi.

The Thomas Carlyle proved to be a period piece of rather a complex sort. The basic idea, clearly, had been a night club with a Victorian *decor*. Had the later nineteenth century achieved the idea of such an institution, its appearance—the proposition seemed to run—would have been like *this*. But *this* had been somewhat uncertainly conceived. There were curtains and heavy furniture that would have satisfied Mr Gladstone, or even the old Queen herself; there was a buffet with young ladies dressed to recall Manet's celebrated picture of the bar at the Folies-Bergère; the walls were lavishly plastered with the work of artists ranging from Landseer and Alma-Tadema to Beardsley and Toulouse-Lautrec; the company sat for the most part at small glass-topped tables upon which some artist of no very refined talent had executed a series of large-scale cartoons of Victorian notabilities. One set down one's glass on Tennyson's nose or tapped one's cigarette-ash into Browning's ear. But the laboured jocularity of all this had itself a period air, and it was necessary to suppose that the Thomas Carlyle was either the recent creation of some elderly person emotionally fixated in the nineteen-twenties, or an actually surviving institution from that conscientiously frivolous era.

Mervyn Twist conducted Judith on her arrival to a table in a corner, where they sat down at opposite

128

ends of the long and lugubrious face of the late Mr
George Moore. At similar tables around them people
were eating oysters or dressed crab, drinking champagne, staring glumly into one another's eyes or va-
cantly into air, and generally behaving in ways
expressive of the hectic night-life of London. In the
middle of the floor a gaunt girl, dressed with ingeniously dissimulated decency in a species of black lace
curtain, plodded her way, unintelligible and disre-
garded, through a succession of French songs.

"Quite, quite absurd," Twist was saying. "And
rather horrible—don't you think? I should suppose
she was as tubercular as an old cow. And look at her
midriff." He glanced uneasily at Judith during these
random remarks, and she supposed that he was ever
so slightly drunk. The girl sang mechanically, like
some contrivance into which a penny has been
dropped.

> *"Papa, je ne comprends pas un mot."*
> *"Ma chère, c'est ce qu'il faut?"*

"Deplorable," Twist said. "Not even honestly *peu-
ple*, not even authentically *canaille*. I expect she's
really quite *bien élevée*, poor little brute. How terrible
life is."

> *"Mais Papa, qu'est-ce ca veut dire?*
> *Moi qui croyais que j'allais rougir."*

The singer had begun to move between the tables,
making perfunctory and conventional gestures of en-
ticement, modesty, lubricity. It could be sketched,
Judith was thinking. But it would need a first-rate

pencil to get in the nullity, the emptiness of the performance. She turned her glance back to Twist. "I don't know that a place like this gives life much of a chance."

"Quite right." Twist gave a nod which was at once emphatic and maudlin. "Most of these people are beyond resuscitation. I can't think why we came."

"Did Gavin Lambert often come? He lived within a stone's throw."

"Look—they've brought us some horrible drink." Twist stared in unnecessary perplexity at the bottle which had been planted on George Moore's drooping moustache. Then he filled two glasses and emptied his at a draught. "Oh, dear, oh *dear*—I believe it's made out of rhubarb. Life *is* grim." Suddenly he looked at Judith in immense surprise. "Do you know? Those were Gavin's last words. Spoken just like that. 'Life *is* grim.' He knew, you know. For he was a great genius. He and I were the only two people who properly understood the—the——" Twist frowned, perplexed. "Do you know—I can't remember what? But something terribly important."

"Would it be the disintegration of reality in the interest of the syncretic principle?"

"That's it. And now there's only me. 'Life *is* grim.' That's what Gavin said. In this very hole. And then he went off and they killed him."

"*Here?*" Judith was startled. "Limbert was here on the night he died?"

"Yes, indeed. It was quite early—some time before those ridiculous police came in. But what has worried me is the hunted man. I've wondered whether I should *tell* the police. But police are so *horrid*." Twist recollected himself. "Except, of course, your hus-

130

band—dear Judith. I'm very fond of Robert."

"John. But who was the hunted man?"

"Somebody Gavin turned out to know. He had an old school tie, and a twisted lip, and he kept on saying that he was a seedy sort of failure——"

"Nonsense. I don't believe a word of it."

"My dear, it is *perfectly* true. I thought he might be a kind of Graham Greene turn put on by this absurd club. I suppose he must have gate-crashed. And he was *tremendously* hunted. Trembling in every limb. And starting at every sound. And looking furtively round. And then Gavin recognised him. They'd been at school together and had even been pals for a bit, because this chap had done a little painting. Gavin got him a couple of drinks."

"Did you discover his name?"

"He was called Crabbe. Or perhaps Crowe or Crewe. At any rate, something *completely* appropriate." Twist drank another glass of the spurious champagne. "Well, they talked for a bit, and then Gavin went away. He only came in here once in a way, and simply to pick up ideas. He didn't drink—not anything to speak of. And when he was going out—just back to his studio, I suppose—he passed by the table where I was sitting. I said something about this Crabbe or Crowe or Crewe looking as if he'd been finding life a bit grim. 'Life *is* grim,' Gavin said—and out he went."

Judith watched Twist refill his glass. "And what happened to Crabbe?"

"He sat for a time at a little table by himself, drumming with his fingers, and glancing first at one door and then the other, and sometimes looking at his watch. He might have been waiting for somebody who had failed to keep an appointment. Sometimes in disgusting places like this you see a man behaving in that way about a girl. Perhaps this really was no more than that. My imagination may have run away with me about that hunted man stuff. My brain is primarily critical and analytic, as you know, dear Judith. But it is powerfully imaginative as well."

"A wonderful combination." Judith looked doubtfully at her entertainer, who was now far advanced in inebriety. A more unreliable informant it would be hard to conceive. But it was no doubt true that on the evening of his death Limbert had been here in the Thomas Carlyle, and had stumbled upon somebody he knew. The incident might well prove to have no significance at all. But John, she knew, would investigate it thoroughly when he got to hear of it. There would have to be questions all round the club. She could scarcely embark upon these herself now, but she must certainly see if there was anything more to be got out of Twist. "And afterwards?" she prompted. "Did anybody turn up on Crabbe?"

"Crabbe?" Twist appeared to be sinking into a state of somnolence. "A delightful poet. So divinely *dreary*."

"Not that Crabbe. The one Limbert met."

"You mean Crewe—or was it Crowe? I really stopped keeping any sort of eye on him. His turn, although *séduisant*, was a shade on the monotonous side. I remember a bunch of people coming in—all men—and his looking up at them sharply, so that I thought they might be what he was waiting for. But when I looked again he had disappeared. And it can have been only a few minutes after that, I suppose, that all those terrible great police arrived. Would you care to dance?"

Judith turned round. The gaunt girl had disappeared and her place had been taken by a band the members of which were disguised as eminent Victorians. Florence Nightingale was at the piano, Cardinal Manning discoursed upon a saxophone, Dr Arnold fiddled, and General Gordon operated a battery of drums. Judith, who found this spectacle markedly unfunny, was about to declare that she *didn't* care to dance, when she found that this was unnecessary. Mervyn Twist had fallen asleep.

To be invited out and then slept on in this fashion, Judith felt, was mortifying to all that is most ineradicable in female vanity. There seemed nothing more to be learnt from Twist, and for wishing him awake rather than asleep she had no rational ground whatever. Nevertheless she found that she was both mildly enraged and slightly at a loss. To slip away seemed ungracious; to lean forward and shake Twist, undignified; to hack at his shins under the table, a shade brutal. She decided on quitting the room for the purpose of powdering her nose. If Twist was still asleep when she came back, she would call it a day and go home.

It was while crossing the room with this programme in view that Judith's eye fell upon a female figure seated alone near the door. It was an odd figure, and ought to have been wholly unfamiliar. For although Judith enjoyed the acquaintance of numerous elderly matrons of ample proportions and stately presence, none of them wore a large and obvious red wig or went about at night in out-size dark glasses. Nevertheless she realised instantly that she knew this person very well, and in a moment she had advanced and put a name to her. "Hullo, Lady Clancarron——"

"*Hist!*" Lady Clancarron extended a monumental arm and drew Judith to a chair beside her. "I am disguised. And recognition would be fatal."

"I see. And I'm so sorry. But I don't think anybody heard."

Lady Clancarron shook her head—cautiously, since she was unused to balancing a wig on it. "In a place like this," she said, "the very walls can hear. If rumour has indeed a thousand tongues"—she paused impressively—"Vice has a thousand ears."

This was a proposition the force of which Judith couldn't quite see. She contrived, however, to resist any impulse to a ribald reply. "You think the Thomas Carlyle very bad? I thought the police had investigated it for you, and found it fairly innocent."

"The police!" Lady Clancarron snorted with contempt. "It's my belief that they are all in the pockets of the Big Interests."

"Really? My husband tells me quite a lot about his work, but he has never mentioned that."

"He is an honourable exception—like the Bishop of London."

Judith was perplexed. "I don't know that John is at all like the Bishop of London."

"Or the Postmaster-General. He is an honourable exception in the government, just as the Bishop is among the clergy. All the others have come to terms with the Monster."

"The Monster?"

"The Moloch. The Web. The Great Conspiracy. The Minotaur of Immorality, bent upon devouring our Young." Lady Clancarron paused in this large rhetoric and leant forward accusingly. "And what," she asked, "are *you* doing here, my child?"

"I certainly haven't come to be devoured." Judith realised that the celebrated moral fanaticism of this old person had reached a stage at which it was over-turning her wits. "And I can't see that the Thomas Carlyle is all that dangerous."

"There are *baths*."

"I beg your pardon?" Judith supposed that she had failed to hear correctly.

"I have discovered that the place has two baths. Why should a haunt of mere dancers and drinkers have that?"

Judith shook her head. "I didn't know, I'm afraid, that baths are so very bad."

"They are an invariable concomitant, child, of the most desperate debauchery. Read Juvenal. Consider Boccaccio."

"Did the police inspect the baths during the raid?"

"They did not. They mishandled the whole matter disgracefully. I watched them at it—from this very chair."

Judith was suddenly interested. "But you weren't *here*, Lady Clancarron? John heard that you were with the inspector controlling the raid, in a police car on the Embankment."

For a moment Lady Clancarron was silent; from behind her fantastic dark glasses she appeared to be glancing warily about her. Then she leant forward and hissed conspiratorially in Judith's ear. "A *ruse de guerre*, child. The person in the car was my maid. And the fool of a policeman didn't know the differ-ence."

135

"But that was magnificent." Judith was genuinely impressed.

The old lady gave a high cackle of mirth that threatened to bring her wig down over one ear. "I was here all the time, and observed the disgraceful way in which the investigation was conducted. I am preparing a report on it—a sensational exposure—for the Home Secretary."

"But if the Home Secretary——"

"I believe that the wretch's days of power are numbered." A positively apocalyptic note came into Lady Clancarron's voice. "It can only be a matter of weeks before the Prime Minister is bound to reorganise his government. And I have it on good authority that the Home Office is to go to the dear Postmaster-General." The old lady made one of her dramatic pauses. "And then the Augean stables will be cleansed."

"Won't that mean you have to find another line?"

"*In part* cleansed. There will always be abundant labour, never fear, for those resolved to combat the Great Pollution. The Sink. The Drain." Rather surprisingly, Lady Clancarron sat back abruptly and reached for a glass. "Have you noticed, child, the abominable quality of the champagne?"

"I certainly have. The drain or the sink is just the place for it."

"Nothing is more infallibly indicative of bad morals than bad champagne."

"Except, of course, baths."

"Precisely. I see that you are a very sensible young person. You must come on our committee."

"About the night of the police raid, Lady Clancarron." Judith's interruption was made in some haste.

"Did you see anybody who might be described as a hunted man?"

"All men are hunted, child. By the Spectre of Vice."

"Of course. But I mean an *actually* hunted man—one who looked as if he were in actual danger from some—some physical pursuit and assault."

"Certainly I did." Lady Clancarron drained her glass almost as rapidly as Mervyn Twist had done, apparently regardless of the acute moral dangers involved. "But that would only be one of the spies."

"One of the spies?" Judith was bewildered.

"Or possibly one of the burglars. I have positive knowledge that spies and burglars make a haunt of this club. And, from time to time, there is a murderer as well. But they are not—are they?—our concern. Our quarry, child, is the Demon of Vice." Lady Clancarron raised a commanding hand. "Waiter," she called sharply, "another bottle."

Judith felt her head gently swim. The old woman was demented. But the mad often notice significant things that the sane ignore. "It doesn't *look* much of a place for criminals," she said cautiously. "I'd call it bourgeois elements having a fling."

"On the night of the raid it was secret agents." Lady Clancarron was now matter-of-fact. "Whether you call *them* criminals is no doubt a matter of taste. I am told that they usually work for both sides indifferently—that to do so is the recognised professional procedure. And that, of course, makes moral judgment a matter of some difficulty. For my own part, I take no exception to secret agents. After a good deal of inquiry, I have satisfied myself that they are a hard working body of men, very little given to sexual depravity."

"I'm very glad to hear it." Judith glanced across the

137

room and saw that Mervyn Twist was still asleep. "But aren't there women spies, who are fearfully glamorous and who——"

Lady Clancarron gave her snort of contempt. "That, child, is only in novels. And even such novels have virtually disappeared. Our Council stamped them out."

"However did it manage to do that?"

"We found that most romances turning upon the activities of seductive women in the pay of foreign powers were the work of elderly spinsters whose vile scribblings scarcely preserved them from the direst penury. So we contacted other charitable bodies and got them places—in homes for aged governesses, and that sort of thing. The result has been the removal of the Shadow of Vice from the spy story. I speak only of this side of the Atlantic, I need hardly say."

"That was very clever." Judith had begun to lose interest in the fantasies of this ancient crusader. She would scribble a note bidding Twist good-night, and then go home.

"Nevertheless, secret agents tend to haunt the same underworld as the Vicious and the Corrupt. I have thus come in the course of my own work to know a good many of them by sight, as well as to recognise the type at a glance. Your hunted man was somebody new. If I had seen him before I should have remembered him. He had a twisted lip."

Judith sat up with a jerk. "Did he appear to be waiting for somebody?"

"Certainly he did. He spent some time talking to a young man whom I judge to have been an artist. But he was uneasy and restless. He hoped for a rendezvous but he feared pursuit or apprehension. Eventually three men entered the room in a group."

"Secret agents?"

"Assuredly. I could not possibly be mistaken about them. Your hunted man looked across at them sharply. He was deciding whether they were on his side."

"But I thought you said, Lady Clancarron, that those people are always on both sides."

"Not necessarily *at once*. They change about. And your hunted man was no doubt deciding whether the newcomers were on his side or the other *then*. His conclusion was plainly adverse. For he got to his feet and bolted out by the other door."

"Looking upset?"

"Naturally." Lady Clancarron was surprised. "He was as pale as death, and so on. No doubt they all went somewhere else and fell to killing each other. The incidence of violent death among secret agents is high. It is one of the things that keep their minds off Sex."

"That is satisfactory, of course. But it is disturbing to think of so much slaughter."

"At least they did not annihilate one another on the evening in question."

Judith looked sharply at Lady Clancarron. "You have seen one of those people since?"

"One of your hunted man's pursuers—if they are to be called that—has been here this evening." From behind her dark glasses Lady Clancarron swept the room. "That is he—just going out now."

139

8

The Thomas Carlyle, Judith decided as she bolted out of it, was not hard to place. It was an ordinary second-rate night club, providing persons of uncertain sophistication and moderate resources with occasional nocturnal amusement more or less on the cheap. Its improprieties were probably seldom either immoralities or illegalities. If it pleased people to dance to the music of a saxophonist disguised as a Prince of the Church, they were free to do so. Perhaps it was up to date. Or perhaps it was very much what another Prince of the Church, as Victorian as Manning and even more Eminent, had described as an uncouth imitation of polished ungodliness. The bees buzzing in Lady Clancarron's bonnet were almost certainly— so far as the Thomas Carlyle went—illusory bees; the Spectre of Vice was here spectral and no more. And so, no doubt, with her burglars and murderers, her spies or secret agents. Through her dark glasses she had decidedly been seeing things.

Yet there had been in the old lady's fantasy one demonstrably substantial element. She had seen what Mervyn Twist had seen: a man with a twisted lip, having the air of a fugitive, impatient about some appointment, and linked—however slightly—to Gavin Limbert. A number of men had come in, and the hunted man—it had been both Twist's phrase and Lady Clancarron's—had looked at them sharply. And there, more or less, the record ended. Only, Lady Clancarron had pointed to one of the men concerned. Judith was hurrying after him now. On the spur of the moment she had turned detective in earnest. She had a hunted man of her own.

He was as yet no more than a close-cropped head of hair, square shoulders in the dark cloth of what was presumably a dinner-jacket, and a rain-coat which he was about to put on before leaving the club. His features were hidden from her, and were he to vanish for five seconds she could not be confident of her ability to recognise him again. Perhaps she ought to confine her ambition to getting a good view of him, so that she would be able to identify him if necessary. Only that seemed a little dull. It would be much more satisfactory to track him down. She doubted whether John would give any large measure of approval to such a project. But one cannot, after all, live in one's husband's pocket all the time.

There was a few seconds' delay in getting her cloak, so that she thought her quarry must elude her at the start. But the man had paused on the pavement immediately outside the club, with an appearance of irresolution. It is the way one behaves—Judith thought—when wondering whether one has waited long enough for a tardy friend. She moved forward so

142

that she could see his face, and then stood by the kerb, as if looking without urgency for a taxi. He was a middle-aged man with small eyes in a round, pale face. It would be possible to feel his aspect as sinister. Perhaps it was no more than this that had set Lady Clancarron at her imaginings.

Rain was falling, and not many people were about. Suddenly the man appeared to come to some resolution. He looked swiftly up and down the street; Judith was aware of his glance pausing on her, ever so briefly, before running on into darkness. He *was* sinister. He had a habit of making warily sure of his surroundings. As a matter of mere routine, he had noted her for future reference. It would be only for a very short distance, she realised, that she could follow him without incurring his suspicion. Now he had turned away and set off at a sharp pace. She waited a moment, crossed the street, and followed on the other side. The man walked on without looking back.

It was time—Judith told herself—to decide what, if anything, all this was about. From Lady Clancarron she had heard a great deal of what was almost certainly nonsense. And, even if not nonsense, it was irrelevant to her own concern at the moment. Secret agents don't steal Old Masters—or at least they are no more in the way of doing so than other among the more adventuresome sections of society. But the old school friend whom Limbert had undeniably met shortly before his death, and the group of men with whom this harried person had been obscurely involved, might well be the thieves, nevertheless. The fact of their having become involved in the fantasies of an eccentric old lady made this neither more nor less probable.

These people had at least been about on the night

on which Limbert was killed—and one of them had been in contact with him. This would constitute a less tenuous link with the Vermeer and the Stubbs if the Vermeer and the Stubbs could be more clearly related to that killing. The outstanding fact about Limbert before his death, surely, was his possession—whether innocently or not—of two stolen paintings, one of them of immense value. Almost certainly the thieves had known where they were; there was no other likely explanation of the conversation and dispute reported by Grace Brooks. Hard upon this Limbert had been killed and his studio ransacked. But both the Stubbs, and the Vermeer as it lay concealed under The Fifth and Sixth Days of Creation, had been untouched. It was only later—on this very afternoon, indeed—that the thieves had got back the Vermeer by raiding the Da Vinci Gallery.

Judith had progressed as far as this in the recapitulation of her problem when she realised that the man she was following had turned down a side-street and disappeared. By the time she had again got him in view he was in the act of making a further turn, and it occurred to her that he was employing himself in simply walking round a block. In this there would be support for the notion that he was still minded to keep some appointment. The road in which she found herself was poorly lit and quite deserted. She proceeded with considerable caution. If the man looked back and was able to distinguish her, he would now at once know that he was being followed.

And probably she was being thoroughly foolish. If the Aquarium had really gone back to old Moe Steptoe, by this time it was almost certainly safe in the hands of the police. John would have seen to that.

And now her quarry had made yet another turn. Three right-angled turns. He could be doing nothing, then, but filling in time. The likelihood was that she had merely put herself on the trail of some innocent amour or vulgar intrigue. This was a most disagreeable reflection, and at the corner she stopped, doubtful about continuing the chase. Before her was another quiet and deserted road, and she scarcely saw how she could continue undetected. Peering down it after the retreating form of the man, she got the impression that it must be a blind alley. An obscure knowledge stirred in her. Her glance went back to the corner, sought and found a street sign. Her whole body stiffened. Gas Street. Gavin Limbert's studio was in Gas Street. In Gas Street he had been killed.

It was, of course, a blind alley—she had been told that. On the right was a line of narrow-fronted houses; on the left, a succession of lower and irregular buildings which had once been stables and now served to house the cars of the more substantial dwellers opposite; ahead, nothing but a brick wall. The Thomas Carlyle lay just beyond that, but whatever back entrance the club possessed did not give on Gas Street. These were observations swiftly made, but Judith had scarcely concluded them when the man in front of her disappeared. He had walked to the bottom of the street and turned straight into the last house. Judith drew a long breath. There *was* a link between Limbert and this man. It could no longer be doubted.

She wished that she could get John on the telephone. She wondered whether she should try to get Cadover. She might wait until the man appeared again—if he did appear—and then endeavour to follow him to wherever it appeared likely that he could be picked up next morning. But she was pretty sure that for this her technique as a sleuth would be insufficient. She could, however, go on and investigate a little further.

Gas Street was deserted. Its farther end looked indefinably uninviting. Although not given to facile alarms, she knew that to take many steps more was to come up against an unknown situation that might be dangerous. And she was not free to flirt with danger. That did not mean, though, that she must be positively panicky. And Judith walked on. The upper end of Gas Street, at least, looked enormously respectable. She would only, she felt, have to give a sufficiently convincing scream to have whole cohorts of the gentlemen of England piling in to her rescue.

It was possibly this pleasing vision that now prompted Judith to a course of action quite as rash as any that—all unknown to her—her husband was more or less simultaneously committing himself to. When she reached the last house in Gas Street and found that the door was open—that it looked, indeed, the sort of door nobody ever shuts—she walked straight in. She would poke about. If challenged, she would claim to be looking for a Miss Arrow. And as Miss Arrow had disappeared on the morrow of Gavin Limbert's death, no positive embarrassment could result. It was true that if she was confronted by the man she had followed, and he recollected having remarked her outside the Thomas Carlyle, a certain awkwardness might ensue. But she could always give that scream.

There was a narrow hall, and a staircase uncertainly lit by gas. Somebody had done a mural on the triangle of wall where the stair mounted. In the air hung a smell of improvised cooking, turpentine, and wet clay stored in bulk. These were all things very familiar to Judith, and she advanced with a new confidence. The sound of voices came through a half-open door on the left. It occurred to her that the man she had been following might be one of the two remaining tenants of the place, either the painter Boxer or the sculptor Zhitkov. If she could verify that, her job for the night would be done. It wouldn't be much of a discovery, but at least it would be something. She advanced to the open door—at any moment she could start inquiring for Mary Arrow—and looked in. Her man was there. The back of his close-cropped head, and his square shoulders, formed a sort of *repoussoir* to the farther recesses of the room. It was, as she had expected, a studio. In the middle of the floor a drawing-board, propped on an easel, showed a rapidly sketched nude, folded up like a concertina so as to yield a rectangular mass, two by one by one. Somebody interested in the possibilities of the double cube. At the far side of the room a massive girl was sitting by a small open fire, stolidly darning a red sock with bright yellow wool. Judith's man was evidently in the position of a caller asking questions. He was being answered with some impatience by another man, at present invisible.

"I tell you, I don't know. And who are you, anyway, and what do you want with him? Does the poor devil owe you money?"

"My name is Cherry." Judith's man answered in a voice so unnaturally soft as to suggest either an excessive desire to mollify or the presence of a markedly psychopathic personality. "I am a friend of his—of Zhitkov's."

147

"Then I'd like to feel your bumps." The invisible man laughed boisterously at this primitive witticism.

"My bumps?" Mr Cherry spoke as if his sex were being mistaken. He was possibly a foreigner and a little at sea with the language.

"Not that I believe a word of it. Zhitkov never had a friend in his life. Not even a shifty, maggot-faced, snooping crawler like Dash Cherry Esquire, who is about to experience the sensation of going through a door on his ear." The architect of this laboriously robust speech now advanced into view, and Judith saw an unshaven man in a blue blouse. He was carrying an empty beer-flagon in a posture of studied belligerence. She supposed that he was rather drunk. "First," he continued, "Grace as a cube goes bust. Then in comes old Inspector Corpse, bringing a ruddy commissionaire in a bowler hat. And now *you*. Well, you may be Cherry. But no tart would look at you."

"Let him be, Boxer." The massive girl by the fire spoke out of what seemed a species of stupor. "He only asked a civil question."

"No more than that, I assure you." Cherry's voice was even softer than before, but Judith now sensed that it was malignant. "Mr Zhitkov made an appointment with me, and then failed to come. So I have come to him. And I only ask when he is likely to be in."

"You can go and wait for him," the girl said. "He never locks up."

"That's right—go and wait for him." The man called Boxer appeared suddenly to have forgotten his animosity. He was staring at his sketch in deep gloom. "Knees to chest and heels to bottom," he said bitterly. "Gives you nothing but curves. It would do for a dirty

148

magazine. Pitiful." He turned to his visitor and waved his arms—quite mildly, as if shooing out a cat. "Off you go," he said. "No need to take two bites at a Cherry. No need to give him the raspberry." But the gentleness of this advance must have been deceptive. Judith became aware that Cherry was either bundling himself or being bundled rapidly out of the room. Her own retreat had to be precipitate, and was made in decidedly poor order.

Judith, in fact, scurried—and moreover scurried in the wrong direction. There was an open door before her, but it was not the outer door of the house. Through it came a flicker of firelight, and she sensed an empty room. At the same moment she heard Cherry recovering his balance in the hall behind her. It became suddenly overwhelmingly important to her that she should not be seen. The feeling, irrational and unexpected, took her through the doorway in a flash. It was another studio—Zhitkov's, of course. In the middle of it she could distinguish in blurred outline a large sculptural mass. She remembered the Venus upon which, to its creator's indignation, there had dripped the blood of Gavin Limbert. Only a few feet above where she now stood, Limbert had been murdered. And from only a few feet above that again, Mary Arrow had disappeared. Was Mary Arrow now a hunted woman—as Crowe or Crabbe or Crewe had been a hunted man? Judith recalled what it was absurd in this moment to have forgotten. She was now a hunted woman herself.

And this ground was dangerous. The mysterious forces that had struck here ten days before were still potentially active and might strike at her too. Something about the man calling himself Cherry had told

149

her that. And Cherry was on her heels now. In a moment he would have come in to wait for Zhitkov. What would happen if—here in the near-darkness—she had to explain herself as waiting for Zhitkov too? There was a step in the passage. The whole place was on so small a scale that everything in it seemed to happen very swiftly. Judith strained her eyes to pierce the gloom of the unfamiliar place. Suddenly they distinguished, not two paces away, an inner door. Perhaps it led to a bedroom. She put out her hand, opened it and slipped through. As she closed the door softly upon herself she was aware of a close, oppressive darkness, and of a queer smell. She guessed that she had shut herself up in what was no more than a large cupboard. Her only companionship was with the depressing knowledge that she had been uncommonly silly.

Footsteps crossed the studio; she heard the scrape of a match; the door concealing her became faintly outlined in streaks of yellow. Cherry had made himself sufficiently free with Zhitkov's quarters to light the gas. A moment later she heard him stir the fire, draw up a chair. She realised with dismay that he was settling in for a long wait. Zhitkov might well have irregular nocturnal habits and not be back for hours. She herself might be stuck in this abominable cupboard for hours. She might even—Judith checked herself. On a rational view there were, after all, limits to the prospect of alarm. She had left John a note that she was going to the Thomas Carlyle. Did she fail to return at a reasonable hour, he would certainly lose no time in making inquiries. Nor would he be long in wondering whether she had, perhaps, made a freakish descent upon the scene of the Limbert mystery.

In the darkness Judith smiled wryly. There were advantages in being pretty thoroughly understood. If she had really got into a mess John would certainly fetch her out of it.

Meantime, she was afraid to move. The space about her was impenetrably black; she sensed it as confined; if she stirred she might bring down anything—tools, plaster casts, Zhitkov's pots and pans. For a little while it was rather fun in its breathless fashion; it recalled the keyed-up, trembling state of some form of hide-and-seek in childhood. Quite soon, though, it would become nervously intolerable.

Judith waited. Nothing happened. She went through a phase of idiotic terror—again like a child, a child who feels that the bolt may have slipped into place on the chest, that a passing servant may have turned the key in the cupboard, that the house—familiar and safe only minutes before—is now empty and that no one will ever come back. The feeling passed, but it left her with an enhanced sense of her own grown-up folly. She knew suddenly that it was due to herself to stop feeling an ass, and that the means to that was stepping out of this absurd lurking-place and confronting Cherry composedly and boldly. She also knew—and with an equal sense of abrupt revelation—that she could do this. The gentlemen of England were up the road and ready to come to her rescue. But, being a lady of England, she was likely to manage a very sufficient rescue of herself.

Buoyed up by this new and exalted view of things, Judith put her hand on the door before her and pushed. Or rather she had given the first hint of pushing when a wholly freakish train of association betrayed her. The ladies of England do not inhabit cupboards. But in Sweden—— What Judith had re-called was that appealing female character of Strind-berg's who lived in a cupboard and believed herself to be a parrot. To Judith in her present situation this suddenly presented itself as being irresistibly funny. She was on the point of laughing aloud—which might have been the best conceivable way of achieving the sudden overthrow of the unsuspecting Cherry—when she heard the door of the studio open. And a new voice said flatly: "Oh—so it's you."

9

Hilarity drained abruptly from Judith Appleby. For the dead-pan voice had added: "What did it feel like—killing Crabbe?"

"Quiet, you fool! Those people across the passage——"

"Boxer?" The new voice was still inexpressive; nevertheless it could be distinguished as foreign, cultivated, precise. "He's drunk. And his packing-case of a model is too stupid to count. But I'll shut the door. There. And now I ask you again, Cherry, how did it feel killing Crabbe?"

"Fine." The soft voice of Cherry was almost caressing. "Almost as fine, Zhitkov, as it felt slugging you."

Zhitkov laughed harshly. "You didn't get much out of it, damn you. And now you think we might talk business, eh? Well, there may be something in that."

"Then why didn't you come to that club as you said?"

"Because, my friend, I didn't choose to. I'm on top, and I mean you to remember it."

"It seems to me that somebody else is on top of both of us. And that's why I think we had better join forces."

Again Zhitkov laughed. "Cherry, you're a fool. You're also a nuisance, it's true, and I might consider buying you off. But don't think we break equal on this. We may both have been left looking silly. But I know things and you don't. And at any moment I'm going to know more. See?"

There was a short silence—perhaps to be interpreted as an acknowledgment by Cherry that he did see. Judith could hear the throbbing of her own heart. The sound was so loud upon her inner ear that she expected both men to turn with one accord to discover what strange engine had begun to beat in the cupboard. There *had* been a man called Crabbe. And he *had* been hunted—hunted to a death which was now matter for hard-boiled talk between these two rival ruffians. For that was what Zhitkov and Cherry appeared to be. What she was listening to was a parley—the tentative and wary discussion of a possible armistice. But for what sort of forces did these men speak? How were they related to the people who had stolen the Vermeer and the Stubbs from Scamnum Court? If Cherry had indeed killed Limbert's old school-fellow Crabbe, how was that killing related to the killing of Limbert? And what did Zhitkov know that Cherry didn't know? Judith felt these and a dozen other new questions pressing upon her with a sort of physical insistence exacerbated by the confinement in which she crouched.

"Crabbe was clever."

154

"Clever—Crabbe?"

"You killed Crabbe, but Crabbe was clever. Clever to the last—that was Crabbe."

Judith wondered if she was falling into the grip of hysteria. For it seemed to her that the voices of the unseen men were falling into a rhythm dictated by her own quickening pulse. Only curiosity, she thought, would enable her to keep her head. If she made an ass of herself now, she would never *know*. Conversely, if she kept her wits about her, a key to the whole mystery might be forged for her in the next half-dozen sentences that Zhitkov and Cherry spoke.

"I can't see Crabbe was all that clever."

"It's your idea that Crabbe had nothing."

"Crabbe had nothing? Crabbe *kept* nothing. All I say is that Crabbe kept nothing. All down the drain."

"All down the drain? Cherry, you *would* think of a drain. You've got a natural nose for a drain."

"Look here, Zhitkov, this won't do. We've got to make a deal."

"We've *got* to make a deal? I like that—we've got to make a deal!"

Judith's head was now swimming badly. And it wasn't because of the talk—the bewilderment of this rapid cross-fire in which it was difficult to follow which of the invisible men said what. And it wasn't the darkness either. It wasn't anything to do with either hearing or seeing. *It was to do with smelling.* The cupboard had a queer, sweet smell—a smell associated with nothing she could think of in an artist's studio. When she discovered this, Judith discovered that she was going to faint. Or at least that she was swaying on her feet. She *must* put her hands out into the darkness and find something by which to support herself; she

155

must do this regardless of any fatal bump or clatter it might occasion. . . .

For one thing, continuing like this was no good. Bodily sensation had got on top of her, and she had stopped being able to follow the sense of what the men were saying. She knew only that they were now talking about the Thomas Carlyle—about something that had happened there, or that ought to have happened there, on that night—the night which was the occasion of all this present horror. . . . Cautiously, without turning her shoulders, she let her right hand grope backwards behind her. Her fingers touched, clutched, moved on, clutched again. They were a sculptor's fingers and she was accustomed to live through them. . . . For a second her mind blacked out. Her first returning knowledge was simply that there was something enormously wrong. She was down on her knees, for one thing. And she must have made a row, coming down like that. Either the men knew, and were simply playing with her, or their dispute had reached such a point of concentration as to make them heedless of the outer world. But all that was unimportant. . . . Her fingers were again out exploring. Her will had not the power to stop them. And again they brought her the same report. She had been brought to her knees among—among——

Perhaps these were only the horrible imaginings of some sudden delirium. Judith tried to bring her mind back to the talk going on in the studio. But that too had gone crazy. Cherry was saying something about a bath. A picture of Lady Clancarron, with her wig crooked over one eye, swam up before Judith, and she had a confused notion that there was something which she ought to connect with something else. The

156

cupboard in which she crouched no longer lay impenetrably dark around her. It was the scene of a queer sort of fireworks. These, she argued to herself, were occasioned by the queer smell. And *that* was occasioned. . . . She thought she heard Zhitkov—or perhaps it was Lady Clancarron—telling her in a loud voice not to empty out the baby with the bath water. She remembered that only a few hours before, she had been bathing her own baby, had been living in a world of complete security and sanity. She must get back to it.

Judith concentrated all her forces, as if for some last and desperate thrust against a formidable barrier. But she knew that it was her fingers that she must use. With an immense effort of will, she once more felt about her. There was something like a breath of cold air in her hair. It flowed over her scalp and down her spine. It drenched her whole body. And to this sensation—for a moment merely physical—she was presently giving a name. It was knowledge—knowledge so grotesque that she ought to be laughing aloud at it. But she had no impulse to do that. For her pulse was dropping to normal and her mind was perfectly clear. Her position must be called hazardous and absurd. It could not be said, therefore, that she was in command of the situation. But she was at least once more in command of herself.

"You know things that I don't? How am I to know there's any truth in that?"

It was Cherry's voice, returning sullenly to some former point in the argument. The two men, it seemed to Judith, had arrived at a deadlock. But if they chose to beat over the whole matter again, that was all to

157

the good. It gave her a second chance, and one which she was now much better able to take.

"Listen, Cherry—I'm not going to give anything away. All you know is this: you stopped Crabbe getting the thing to me—stopped him by killing him. But you suspect I *must* have got it, after all—for where else could it have got to? Well, you're right. And you're also wrong." Zhitkov gave his harsh laugh as he propounded this conundrum. "Crabbe kind of got it to me—and then others stepped in."

"What others could step in? You're trying to fox me, Zhitkov. There aren't another others that knew. First your lot got the thing. Then my lot got to know, and I played my hand. I admit I came down on it. But there *were* only our two lots. No other lot *could* know." Cherry was again soft, repetitive, obstinate.

"You're quite right. Nobody else did know. But somebody else stepped in, all the same."

"Who else stepped in?"

"Steptoe stepped in—or that's my guess."

"What's that you say? You're talking gibberish. You're wasting my time."

"That's right, Cherry—I'm wasting your time." Zhitkov gave his ugly laugh, and Judith wondered if her head was going to start swimming again in the effort to find sense in what she was listening to.

"How could Crabbe, as you say, kind of get it to you?" Once more Cherry had gone doggedly back.

"There was the telephone, wasn't there? Cherry, you're a fool. I always thought so: Cherry is a fool."

"There was the telephone? What about the telephone? Crabbe couldn't get you *that* on the telephone."

"He could tell me a lot—all I had to know. But

158

Crabbe couldn't tell me what he didn't know himself. About the stepping in of Steptoe—the unknown factor in the whole affair."

"*There's* the telephone."

A bell was ringing sharply somewhere in the studio. It was out of place, Judith thought—a telephone in a studio like this. But then Zhitkov, decidedly, was not what he seemed. She had learnt that much, at least. . . . For some seconds the bell continued its insistent summons. Zhitkov, she guessed, had no great fancy for taking the call in Cherry's presence.

"Go on, Zhitkov—perhaps it's Crabbe." Cherry was softly mocking. "Perhaps it's Crabbe, and he'll be telling you things. News from hell."

"*You* go to hell."

The bell went silent. Zhitkov must have picked up the receiver. And in a second he said sharply: "Speak low." There was an interval of silence. Then his voice rose a pitch, excited and furious. "Didn't get it . . . you say you didn't get it? You say *they* got it . . . what do you mean? Did you say a fight—a fight in the shop? It proves I was right, but you ought to have got it. . . . Tell me about that. . . . It must have been Cherry's men—and Cherry's here now. . . . You're sure of that? What about speed? . . . I said, what about speed? They wouldn't have speed in a thing like that? What about the dark? You can often be given the slip in the dark. Remember Crabbe. . . . I said, remember Crabbe. . . . If they just hold on. They *must* hold on."

The receiver went down with a click. There was silence again. Judith knew that it was the silence of quite a new tension in the room.

"You clever devil." It was Zhitkov. His voice had

159

changed. "You knew. *You* knew about this man Steptoe and his lot."

"Ah—Steptoe. You were speaking about Steptoe." Cherry was softer than ever—and non-committal, enigmatic. "And you thought that our lot didn't know about Steptoe."

"You've been working fast." There was reluctant admiration in Zhitkov's tone. "It was only to-day that *I* saw the truth. It was only to-day *I* tracked Steptoe down. We waited for the dark. That would be the time to collect the picture——"

"Ah!" Cherry's interruption seemed involuntary. "So it would."

"There had been a fight—Steptoe knocked silly. And Steptoe's shop knocked silly too. A van moving off. We've just got on to it. We're following it now. That would be you."

"It wasn't me. And the fight wasn't me." Cherry spoke more rapidly than he had done so far, as if he was aware that some critical moment had come.

"Not you? Then Steptoe's own lot——"

"I suppose so. But whoever it is, your people are following?"

"Yes."

"In that green Humber?"

"What do you know about that green Humber?" Once again Zhitkov's voice had risen sharply.

"It's been one of our lines on you, Zhitkov, you fool. And whatever you're trailing, we're trailing too."

"You're trailing the Humber?"

"We never let up on trailing the Humber. What about talking?"

"I think we'll talk." There was a sound of movement, and Judith guessed that both men were now

160

standing up. "But the talking had better be—you know where. Let's get along."

"Let's get along."

In some queer way the relationship between Zhitkov and Cherry had been transformed. And for some further reason—equally obscure—the change seemed to necessitate a changed venue for their further parley. Almost before Judith was aware of what had happened, they had left the studio and she was alone.

It was only when she got outside the cupboard that she realised how bad that smell had been. No wonder that it had set her imagining things. Zhitkov must have lowered the gas as he went out; she turned it up again and went back to stare at her late prison. It was very like what, in the stifling darkness, she had fancied it to be: a charnel-house of decomposing flesh. There, sure enough, was the litter of dismembered limbs over which her horrified fingers had passed; and it was from these that the smell came. Fascinated, she went up and touched them once more. They had a rubbery consistency—it wasn't like living flesh, but it was decidedly like—— At one and the same time Judith laughed and shuddered. The experience was now ridiculous, but it had been sufficiently real. Zhitkov did actually have this profession. He modelled in queer new stuffs with a filthy smell—commercial modelling, it looked like—and this cupboard was a dump or store.

But Zhitkov was something else. And *primarily* something else. Both his racket and Cherry's were organised affairs established on a big scale—Cherry's, it seemed, on a bigger scale than Zhitkov's—and in a more or less permanent way. . . . Judith recalled the International Society for the Diffusion of Cultural Objects—that ramifying organisation built up to trade in Europe's post-war vanished works of art. She recalled what John had told her of a no less astonishing or nefarious group—that of the Friends of the Venerable Bede. She recalled too the abominable scoundrel Wine, who had amassed the power to carry off from their rightful owners not mere pictures and statues but objects as miscellaneous as a Bloomsbury house, a Harrogate cab-horse, and a classical case of multiple personality in a seventeen-year-old girl. It was with criminality on a similar scale—if directed to some quite different end—that she appeared to be in contact now. And John was in contact with it too. . . . She frowned, obscurely disturbed.

John would be home by now. He had gone off to deal with old Moe Steptoe, who had almost certainly become again possessed of the stolen Vermeer. How John had intended to proceed, she had not inquired. He had simply taken hat and coat and walked out of the house, leaving her to entertain the Duke of Horton until that nobleman thought proper to betake himself to his hotel. But, whatever had happened, John should certainly be home by this time. And Judith turned to hurry out. She could get a taxi at the top of Gas Street; and she had news which, however confused and fragmentary, might be useful. Moreover she had no wish to linger in Zhitkov's studio a moment longer than she need help. The place had given her some moments so nasty that she would always shudder at the memory of it. And—quite apart from that— Zhitkov might come back at any time—either alone, or with Cherry again, or with some group of his own circle of ruffians.

But suddenly Judith was so impatient, so irrationally apprehensive, that she could not feel even a taxi to be half quick enough. Her glance went to Zhitkov's telephone. Why not risk using that? Once she had reported herself to John she would be safe.

She went rapidly to the instrument, picked up the receiver, and dialled her own number. Long before there was an answer she had to acknowledge a mounting sense that something was wrong. If John was at home—and even if he had gone to bed and fallen asleep—he would have answered by now. . . . When a voice did come it was a woman's—the sleepy voice of her only resident domestic. Sir John had not come in.

Judith rang off—and for some seconds stared blankly at the bloated volumes of the London telephone directory. Why was this information so unaccountably disturbing? There was no reason why John, once personally involved with the job, should not spend the whole night happily clearing up on the Vermeer affair. . . . Only it was not ten minutes since she had heard Zhitkov receiving something that sounded like the latest report from a battle-front. Steptoe's shop, late that night, had become the focus of interest for obscurely conflicting criminal forces. There had been a fight in it. There had been no indication that police were now in possession, or that they had been involved or invoked at any stage. . . . Judith, upon a sudden impulse, seized a volume of the directory and rapidly turned its pages.

And there was no reply from Old Moe's shop. The telephone didn't even ring there; she could get nothing but the low burr announcing that a number is unobtainable. But there was always the possibility that she had unconsciously dialled the wrong number. She tried again, and with the same result. She was about to put back the receiver for the second time when the instrument crackled oddly. It was a sound she did not remember hearing before; it faded slightly and then remained continuous. She guessed at some technical fault—and guessed too that despite this she had after a fashion got through. She waited for a voice that didn't come. "Hullo," she said. "Hullo, is that Mr Steptoe?" And now there was a reply—but of a sort to make her persuade herself that her ear had betrayed her. "Is that Mr Steptoe?" she said again. Once more she heard the same sound. There could be no mistaking it. It was a low groan. And a moment later there was a clatter, as if the distant receiver had tumbled from nerveless fingers to the floor. The instrument went dead.

Judith had supped enough with horrors for that night. She flicked down the receiver rest and dialled another number. This time it was Whitehall 1212.

Rain was pattering down outside. Through it Judith fancied she could hear, very faintly, the Eminent Victorians doggedly making night hideous with their swing and jive. Or perhaps it was just a radio further up Gas Street. She couldn't be certain of the direction. And she couldn't be certain of a lot of more important things. What she had to say would be a muddle. And it wouldn't even be to John that she would be saying it. . . .

She sat down. She felt very flat. Appeal to the police and they make you feel like that—quite safe but very flat. She had been told to wait. There had been no suggestion that she should seek the protection of Boxer, or hide in a cellar, or arm herself with a poker.

That wasn't carelessness; it was simply an index of the complete efficiency and confidence of the powerful machine she had invoked. Yes, madam, we'll come at once. Lady Appleby? Thank you, madam.... The voice had been quite unimpressed.

And here was an ordinary, shabby studio, with a bad piece of carving in the middle of the floor and a lot of commercial stuff hidden away in a cupboard. Over the way was Boxer—either asleep, or sobering up, or getting a little drunker than he had been. Up above, there was an empty flat. And up above that, another empty flat. Puzzle flats. Problem flats. Think about those flats and you cease to feel flat. You know that you haven't been imagining things, like poor old Lady Clancarron. There really is a Limbert mystery, and you are in on it. And there is a Mary Arrow mystery, too. A shy girl, that. She won't come out of the wings. Perhaps she is going to be the goddess in the machine—descending, not without some audible creaking of ropes and pulleys, to tidy things up in the last act.

But the police wouldn't be interested in a neat literary allusion. They were on their way now, and Judith had better try to do a little tidying up herself. What had she heard in this room that really added to knowledge on the affair? What did she now know that she wished John knew?

Steptoe had stepped in. Zhitkov had let that out in the first instance simply because the jingle amused him, and because he believed he could afford a little mockery of Cherry. Well, begin with it. If Steptoe had stepped in, that meant that he, and the associates with whom clearly he was provided, had not been the prime movers in the affair. And there were consid-

165

erations that leant support to the probability of that. Old Moe, surely, with his junk shop and his petty receiving of stolen goods and constant brushes with the police, was not a criminal on a large scale, or with the sort of resources and knowledge that could organise the elaborate business of the Spanish chest that had been sent to the Duchess of Horton. All *that* had been contrived by others—and then old Moe had stepped in. Whereupon Gavin Limbert had stepped in upon old Moe. And after that——Judith frowned, fearful that her mind was going to waver helplessly before the complexity of the thing—to admit that here was a mystery for the solving of which a professional was needed. And after that yet another set of rascals had stepped in. Or at least here was the general formula for the affair. Crooks all over the place—and biting each other. Three rival shows. Quite prepared to talk things over among themselves. That was what she had just been listening to. But equally prepared for a little slugging—Zhitkov had been slugged—or even for a little murdering—Crabbe had been murdered, and Limbert had been murdered too.

Crabbe had been Zhitkov's man and Crabbe had been clever. He had been clever because he had got something to Zhitkov over the telephone. There didn't *sound* as if there was anything very clever in that; Judith herself had just used the telephone to get something over to Scotland Yard. Perhaps there had been a code, and Crabbe had got a message away within the hearing of his unsuspecting enemies. Yes, perhaps it had been something like that. . . .

It didn't take one very far. Cherry had believed that *Crabbe kept nothing*. And Crabbe had *kind of got* something to Zhitkov—and then *others stepped in.*

That meant Steptoe and his friends. They, so far as both Cherry and Zhitkov were concerned, were *the unknown factor in the whole affair*. Or were they? Judith realised that she was guessing.

And she could only guess. No satisfactory theoretical construction was possible to her, because her information was too fragmentary, too confused. But she did possess a fairly clear picture of one concrete situation—a situation existing *now*. A van had got away from Steptoe's. And it had got away *with* something: presumably the Vermeer. On the whole, she had gathered that it was Steptoe's van; that Steptoe's associates still controlled the booty. Zhitkov's friends had arrived on the scene just too late for effective action, but they were trailing the van in a green Humber. And Cherry in his turn was having the Humber trailed. This last circumstance appeared to have impressed Zhitkov; to have given him a new view of his opponents' reach and tenacity. As a result of it he had shown signs of coming to terms with Cherry, and it was on something like that understanding that the two had gone off together. . . . And that was about all Judith knew. Somewhere in the night that queer multiple chase was going forward.

She had left a piece out. She had left it out because—obscurely—she had wanted to ignore it. There had been a fight at Steptoe's. *And that had been John*. The knowledge came to her, intuitively and absolutely, as she stared blankly at the wretched piece of carving upon which, to the affected indignation of the bogus sculptor Zhitkov, Gavin Limbert's life-blood had dripped.

The bare floor was moving under her oddly, was flowing beneath her like a river. Without knowing it,

167

she had sprung to her feet and was running for the door. They ought to be here by now. By now the big, dark, discreet car should have swept round the corner of Gas Street, past the prosperous and tasteful dwellings of all those gentlemen of England, and be here at the door of this shabby, tragic and enigmatical place.

She was out in the darkness of the little hall. It was unrelieved by any glint of light from Boxer's door, so presumably he had gone to bed. The house and the street were both quite silent except for a continued light drum and patter of rain. She could no longer even fancy that she heard dance-music from the Thomas Carlyle. But suddenly, standing tensely there and straining her ears for the hum of an engine, she did hear something. It was the sound of a key—turning in a lock upstairs.

10

The tiny sound was a challenge. It was a challenge because it was frightening, and it was frightening because it was tiny. Judith was never to get further than this in explaining to herself what she now did. A revolver-shot, a cry, the sound of a heavy fall: any of these would have scared her in her present situation, and sent her precipitately out into Gas Street looking for that overdue police car. What she had in fact heard—this scarcely distinguishable click of a key turning, once and once only, in its accustomed wards—came to her, for some occult reason, as far more alarming than that. And at once she turned towards it as if she were no more than the needle on a delicate acoustic instrument. She turned and went up the stairs in the darkness, past the invisible mural with its London policemen blasphemously posed, up to where she had never been except in imagination, up to Gavin Limbert's studio.

The sound of the turning key, she realised, had

169

operated like a symbol; it had been the very signature of a man returning home. A scratch or scrape, a fumble, would have given quite a different impression, been wholly without power to give that particular prick of fear. But the practised movement, the one deft twist that said *Home*——

She was going up fast, and in total darkness. Anything—a cat, a milk bottle, an unexpected twist on the stair—might have brought her down with a bump, painfully and ridiculously bruised. But it didn't occur to her that it is usually with the aid of some sort of light that one undertakes to mount a strange staircase. She went up without consciousness of muscular effort, as if on an escalator. On the first-floor landing she expected a square of light, and beyond it a dead man pottering idly in his own room. . . .

But that was absurd, and of course there was only more darkness. Judith felt cautiously about her. It was a restricted space. Very soon her hands had travelled all over it. There was only the one door, and that was firmly locked. Moreover the whole place had a deserted feel. Under her fingers she could sense the film of dust which had begun to accumulate as soon as Limbert died. She had played herself a foolish trick in imagining that turning key.

Suddenly she became aware of movement somewhere above her head. It was a movement only of light—a broadening beam of light through an opening door. There was another flat; she remembered that she had forgotten that. Mary Arrow's flat. She turned her head and looked up the further narrow staircase. The light was a feeble one. But she could distinguish in it a pair of trousered legs, standing quite still on

170

the upper landing. Then a deep voice said, "You'd better come up."

And again Judith climbed. When she got to the landing the legs had disappeared. But there was an open door. Through it she heard the faint hiss of a gas lamp and the stronger hiss of a gas ring. She walked straight across the threshold into a sparsely furnished room. A woman of about her own age, dressed in black corduroy slacks and a grey jersey, was standing before the empty fireplace. Her face was drawn and haggard, with dark rings under the eyes, and her body beneath its mannish clothes could be discerned as nerveless and limp. The woman was either sick, or exhausted, or worn down by some stubborn despair. And the woman took one look at Judith and said in her deep voice, "I don't know you. But you look ill, or desperately worried, or tired out."

Judith was able to laugh—weakly but without incivility, for the woman in slacks had disappeared into a small kitchen. "I'm only just home," her voice said. "I've done no more than change into these pants and put on a kettle. It must be late. But not too late for a cup of tea."

"Home? Are you Miss Arrow?"

"That's right." There was a pause, and the sound of boiling water hissing into a teapot. "Are you somebody looking for Gavin?"

Judith felt an odd pricking sensation in her spine. "No," she said. "I wasn't looking for Mr Limbert. I know about——"

"He doesn't seem to be in." Mary Arrow had reappeared, carrying a tray; she seemed to accept Judith's

171

visit as wholly natural. "I gave a bang on his door as I came past. No reply."

Judith had been standing in the middle of the room. Now she very much felt that she wanted to sit down. For this she had recourse to the nearest object, which was a music-stool. "Have you——" She hesitated. It had been her intention to add "been away long?" But even this oblique approach appeared insufficiently cautious in face of the queer situation confronting her. "Have you really made tea for me too? That's very kind."

Mary Arrow set down the tray on the room's only table, and then looked at it as if she were seeing it for the first time. "Tea," she said. "Yes—tea."

"It looks delicious." The idiocy of this remark—for there was, after all, nothing to see except a pot and two cups—at once struck Judith as an index of her own sense of discomfort. "I adore tea at night." She could do no better before this obscurely distraught woman, it seemed, than bolster up one silly piece of gush with another. Mary Arrow herself had made a much better show. She had said, "I don't know you. But you look ill."

"I wonder if Gavin would like to come up? But I forgot—he's out." She stood with the teapot poised in air. "Gavin's out," she repeated. Her deep voice had gone dull, as if she were bent on concealing from herself her own bewilderment, or desperation.

"You know Gavin Limbert well?" Judith, coming to a straight question, looked Mary Arrow straight in the eyes. She saw there something that she didn't like seeing: a flicker of terror, or of pain. But she began to feel less inadequate, all the same.

"We are lovers—but hardly anybody knows." The

172

woman handed Judith her cup, and as she did so her tired eyebrows momentarily contracted themselves in perplexity. "I wonder why I tell you that? It isn't a thing I like or go in for—the frank and doggy attitude."

"I'd guess it wasn't."

"However, there it is. Two flats, and a fire-escape in between. Gavin likes concealment. He says it's something about considering old-fashioned relatives. Actually, it's something in his nature. But he doesn't know that." The woman frowned again, put up a hand as if to clasp her forehead in distraction, checked the gesture and smoothed her hair. "Yes, I *am* talking strangely to-night . . . I think I've been ill." She looked uncertainly at Judith. "Forgive me. Are you somebody I ought to know?"

"I'm quite a stranger, I'm afraid. My name is Judith Appleby."

Mary Arrow shook her head. "That must be right. I'm sure I don't know a Judith. Shall I call you Judith? It's the habit round here."

"Please do." Judith paused. "Where have you just come from, Mary?"

Mary Arrow made as if to speak, checked herself, turned away and crossed the room. She came back holding an open tin. "A few ginger snaps left," she said, and gazed straight over Judith's head. She had executed some mysterious retreat.

But Judith tried again. "What have you been doing to-day?"

"Oh, this and that." Mary's voice had taken on a pathetic disguise of boredom, of indifference. "And you?"

"Shopping. Then I lunched with my husband." It occurred to Judith that a matter-of-fact recital might

173

help. "And then we both went on to a private view."

The effect of this was extraordinary. Mary Arrow flushed—it was like the blush of a girl—and her whole body trembled. She sat down, with her eyes now fixed on Judith's face. "There's something Gavin and I call that—a private view."

Judith was silent. But she guessed that this wasn't going to be crudely embarrassing. It was going to be something critical for the queer mental state with which she was in contact.

"Peeping into his studio from the fire-escape. There are holes in the shutters. You see?" The almost meaningless question was desperately urgent.

"I see."

"When I was first in love with Gavin, and before he had thought about me at all, I used to do that. Perhaps it was dishonourable, or improper or indecent—I don't know. It was just to watch him working—sometimes late into the night. And afterwards of course I told him. And we called it my private view. I went on doing it sometimes—just for fun." The distraught woman before Judith was now in the throes of an uncontrollable agitation. "And we still call . . . we *still* call——"

Judith, listening to Mary Arrow's deep, slow sobs, wondered if the police car had come. And she found that she wanted five, ten minutes grace. A doctor, perhaps nurses, would be needed; she was very sure of that. But for the moment she wanted nothing official or heavy-footed in the room. Fate had brought her to this woman in this moment, and it was up to her to go through with it herself. It was like the sleuthing she had attempted earlier than night. She didn't know the technique, and she might well come a cropper.

174

But even without knowing whether the right thing was to be slow or sudden, sympathetic or impersonal, gentle or incisive, she must have a go. She got up, went round the table, and put an arm on Mary Arrow's shoulder. "Mary," she said, "this is no good. You know it's no good. Everything is coming back, everything must come back. It's coming back now only because you're strong enough for it. Think. There's one thing you must face. What is it?"

"Gavin's dead."

The admission had come with the effect of being dredged up from an immense depth. Or it was like a birth. Mary Arrow was lying back in her chair, trembling but relaxed, sweat on her forehead, but with a sort of peace achieved. Prosaically, like an old midwife, Judith poured her out another cup of tea.

"It's all I remember—that Gavin's dead. He's not downstairs at all. It was stupid to knock on his door. As stupid as knocking on a grave. . . . *You* knew he was dead?"

"Yes."

"Yesterday?"

"He—he died ten days ago."

"I don't remember. I don't remember anything. I must have lost my memory." For a moment, and with an effect of the grimmest comedy, a look of large surprise replaced the stupefied grief on Mary Arrow's face. "I never thought those things really happened."

"I believe they do—even to people who have never shown any sign of anything of the sort. There have been all sorts of fantastic cases of loss of memory. My husband has told me about them." Judith had a feeling that talk, somehow, was useful, was serving to re-create a normal and solid environment for Mary. "His

175

work has brought him into contact with that sort of thing."

"You are married . . . Judith? To a doctor?"

"Not a doctor. My husband's a policeman."

"I don't believe that." Mary's voice was uneasy, and she looked at Judith with something like swift reproach. "That's the worst of being ill—ill in the head. People talk rubbish to you."

"I'm sorry, Mary. It's a way we have of speaking. My husband is responsible for the C.I.D. at Scotland Yard."

"Now you're talking." Something like a tiny bubble of humour rose and broke on the surface of Mary Arrow's mind. "You look as if you might belong to that sort of person, Judith. And I don't belong to anybody at all. It's pretty grim." Mary's face was going white. "And it seems I wasn't able to take it—Gavin's death. That's stupid, I suppose. Other women's lovers have died, and they haven't made show pieces of themselves, to be docketed and chatted over by policemen." Her voice failed and she wept again. Judith remained silent; she knew that now there was no need to break in. And presently Mary raised her head. "I'm sorry I said that about chatting policemen. I expect your husband's all right, Judith."

"Yes—he's all right. Only——"

Powerfully there had come back to Judith a sense in which her husband might not be all right. Mary Arrow's lover had been brutally killed—as a mere move, it seemed, in an obscure battle into which John had thrown himself now. For a moment she forgot Mary Arrow and her grief, and sat in frozen panic. She found that the sense of time had deserted her; the police car might have been delayed for hours; she

176

might have been struggling with this stricken woman for hours. She looked across at Mary, and felt compunction for her own impatience, her own absorption in a mere nervous anxiety. For Mary's flicker of vitality had gone out again; she looked as if she had once more turned away from struggle; she looked like a mere piece of machinery that has run down for the last time. She could be roused again. There was little doubt about that. But somebody would have to work at it—quite hard.

Judith raised her head. There were voices down below, footsteps, a measured knocking at a door. And the knocking sent her blood racing strangely. Order, security, swift and effective action were coming back with that knock. The footsteps sounded on the stairs, the knocking was repeated almost at her elbow, there were uniformed policemen in the room. Behind them came a figure in plain clothes—clothes which showed evidence of having been hastily put on in some suburban dormitory. And now Detective-Inspector Cadover was looking at her with evident relief—and with equally evident disapproval. It was only a question of whether he would blow her up now, or wait and take it out of John—respectfully but implacably.

She jumped to her feet. Mary Arrow looked up at her—apprehensive but also dazed and listless. "Judith," she asked, "who are they? What is it?"

Gently, Judith took her by the arm. "It's the world getting going again, Mary. It has to."

11

"A *green* Humber?" Cadover scribbled notes
as Judith talked, and constables took them out of the
room.

"Yes. Zhitkov said his people were following the
van, and Cherry rather scored over him by showing
he knew it would be in a green Humber."

"It's not the most common of colours, and that's
something. We're sure to pick it up by daylight,
but with luck we'll have it long before then. And the
fellow who called himself Cherry, Lady Appleby—
he hinted that his people were in turn following the
Humber?"

"Yes."

"But he didn't say what in, or on?"

"No. He wasn't giving anything of that sort away.
It was what impressed Zhitkov—the discovery that
Cherry's people were right on top of his. He seemed
to decide that he must come to an agreement with

Cherry, after all. And it was then that they went away together."

Cadover looked at his watch. "That was nearly an hour ago. They may be slugging each other again by now. I wouldn't give much for their precious agreement." He scribbled another note. "An hour's a long spell for a patch of honour between thieves."

Judith looked across the bare room at Mary Arrow. "You think they are thieves? I can't understand it. They seem so—so unnaturally thick on the ground."

"It's a big affair, Lady Appleby. I've known rival gangs cutting each other's throats over hauls far less considerable than this of one of the world's most valuable pictures. And now I think we'd better be getting along."

Judith had thought of Detective-Inspector Cadover as a slow-moving and even somewhat ponderous man, but now she was becoming disabused of this notion. Making notes on one pad, scribbling and detaching a stream of messages on another, asking questions and weighing answers, he even had some reserve of mental energy for the framing of occasional moral sentiments. She wondered whether he was anxious about John. Certainly he showed no signs of it. Now he had stood up, and appeared to be sparing a moment for a glance of disapproval—perhaps ethical, perhaps aesthetic—at Mary Arrow's black slacks. Judith stood up too. "What about Miss Arrow?" she asked. "She can hardly be left here."

"I suppose not." Cadover spoke as if this were striking him for the first time. It seemed that he had a little to spare too for a very private fun. "No—it would hardly do."

"I thought perhaps I might take her home with me."

"That's an excellent suggestion, Lady Appleby." Cadover scribbled another note and handed it to a sergeant beside him. He was like a celebrity, Judith thought, giving autographs. "She still seems very distraught. Perhaps you'd get her down to the car." He turned and rattled out a quick series of commands to a man standing at the door. "A woman's touch," he added. "A true solace on sad occasions like this. See if you can put her into a coat. And her bag, Lady Appleby, if you can find it. Powder, lip-stick—that sort of thing. They talk better when they can do a bit in that way. . . . You, my man—don't stand about like a fool."

"Talk?" Judith was startled. "I'm sure she's not fit to talk. The first thing I shall do is to call a doctor."

"Fishguard." Cadover had swung round on another of his assistants. "I never like to have Fishguard forgotten. Quite as important as Holyhead or Liverpool or Heysham. . . . A doctor is a very good idea, Lady Appleby. And now we'll go down. The cars are waiting."

They went down. And once more Judith had no consciousness of muscular effort in treading Mary Arrow's staircase. Only, this time, the effect was less of being on an escalator than on a conveyor belt. And Cadover, she felt, now had similar conveyor belts in operation all over the south of England. . . . Gas Street was still ill-lit and silent. She could hear no waft of music from the Thomas Carlyle, so perhaps it had packed up for the night—or for the morning. Possibly the place was scared of another raid, for there were certainly plenty of police in evidence. Two big cars

181

had been turned about, and were facing up the street with their engines running. She had the impression that in the more respectable stretch of Gas Street a good many doors and windows were open, and that people were peering out to see what was up. She heard further swift, unhurried conference in the darkness around her, and then she was sitting beside Cadover in a big, dark car. They were moving. "But Mary," she said. "She ought to be in here."

"Miss Arrow? I've put her in the other car, Lady Appleby. On second thoughts, she'll be better going straight to the Yard."

Judith was indignant. "But you said I could——"

"It was your remark about a doctor, ma'am." When Cadover used this form of address Judith knew he was adamantine. "Most judicious. And at the Yard there'll be a doctor on call. With wide experience of these distressing conditions."

"But I ought to be——"

Cadover had leant forward in the darkness, picked up an instrument and begun to speak into it. She supposed it to be some sort of radio. Perhaps he was talking to the people in the second car—or perhaps he was telling Liverpool that he judged it of no more importance than Fishguard. She sat back, feeling helpless. But now he was again addressing her. "Of course, I hope you'll come to the Yard too. No reason why you shouldn't be with Miss Arrow if you care to. And we'll be back there within half an hour. Just a bit of a detour to make first."

"Thank you. I'll certainly come. . . . Do you think my husband may be there, Inspector?"

"Sir John hasn't been in to the Yard, Lady Appleby. And he hasn't contacted any police station to-night.

182

But if he does so now—anywhere in the country—I shall know within ten minutes."

"I see." In the darkness Judith looked straight at this news. "John is still terribly fond of having a go on his own."

"To be sure, Lady Appleby. And I don't blame him." Cadover spoke rather in the fashion of an indulgent parent. "Dreary work, sitting at a desk." He paused, as if seeking to amplify this statement. "All work and no play, makes Jack a dull boy. . . . Not, of course"—he seemed anxious that no wrong interpretation should be set on this remark—"that Sir John ever gets precisely *dull*. Far from it. . . . But here we are. If you don't mind just waiting for ten minutes in the car——"

"Where are we?"

"Steptoe's junk shop, Lady Appleby."

"I'm coming in."

"If you don't mind, ma'am——"

But this time Judith resolved to dig in her heels. "Moe's an old acquaintance of mine, Inspector. I might help. I'm coming in."

Old Moe Steptoe was not in very good trim for receiving visitors. He lay on an ancient horsehair sofa with three legs—like a study in sordid realism, Judith thought, that the painter had disposed at some modish tilt in relation to the main planes of his picture. And the horsehair itself, exuding through half a dozen rents in the sofa, gave him an inhuman appearance, as of some exotic creature oddly patched with curly excrescences. It was clear that one of Cadover's conveyor-belts had already reached his shop, for a police sergeant and a constable were brooding over Moe in marked perplexity, one at his head and one at his heels. The total effect was reminiscent of a grotesque heraldic device. There ought—Judith rather wildly thought—to be a motto underneath. It would have to be a Latin pun on old Moe's name—something like that. "Is he hurt?" she asked.

"Something shocking." The sergeant shook his head gravely. " 'Orrible savagery, marm." And he turned to Cadover. "I didn't think, sir, there was a gang left in London that did this sort of thing. And the shop—well, you'll 'ave seen for yourself, sir, as you came through. Reminds me of the old doodle-bug days, it does. Grave and malicious damage to property, they'll bring that in. Like a bull in a china shop, in a manner of speaking. That's what I said to the constable 'ere, as soon as we stepped through the door. Like a bull in a china shop."

Cadover received this with an unflattering growl. "It's a junk shop, man, not a china shop. And most of the damage was done to the stuff fifty years ago. Still"—and Cadover could be seen bringing a massive fairmindedness into play—"it's a remarkable sight, I quite agree. . . . And what's the matter with *him*?" He pointed with marked lack of sympathy at Steptoe. "Shot?"

"No, sir. It's contusions. Multiple contusions on the 'ead. We found him lying by his telephone. Banged about, you might say, by a whole 'orde of savages. The surgeon's been sent for."

"Very proper. But while we wait for him we can get on with our business well enough. The man's conscious, sergeant. He's been making a fool of you. Now then"—and Cadover gave old Moe a brisk shake—"you're not on your death-bed, my man, and you

184

know it. So you can sit up and give an account of yourself."

Steptoe stirred and gave a faint groan.

"We've no time for theatricals. Somebody get a bucket of water and send it over him. That should bring his wits back."

Steptoe groaned again—but this time much more loudly.

"Got it, sergeant? Right over his head."

With ludicrous abruptness, old Moe sat up. "It's assault," he said. "Where's my lawyer? I'll have damages."

"You'll need your lawyer, all right. And he'll have to be a smart one." Cadover looked grimly at the revived antique dealer. "Now then, what's been happening here? Who attacked you?"

"That was the police too. A brutal and unprovoked attack upon a respectable trader. And damage to a valuable stock-in-trade. And bringing a high-class and old-established business into notoriety and disrepute."

"This is a very serious allegation—and not at all likely to lighten your load of troubles. Will you be good enough to tell me what police officer you charge with assaulting you in this way?" Cadover was breathing hard. "And would you undertake to identify him?"

"Of course I would. I've seen his photograph a dozen times. Your boss—that's what he is. Name of Appleby. Sir Bloody-something-or-other Appleby."

Could old Moe, in the present depressed posture of his affairs, have taken any pleasure in producing a sensation, that pleasure would undoubtedly have been his. The several officers of the police grouped around him registered various degrees of indignation

185

and shock. Cadover took a step backwards and eyed him narrowly. And Judith Appleby cried out, "John— my husband? What do you mean?"

"I mean what I say—see? Appleby tried to murder me. And that's a serious thing. For no reason at all, it was. Or none to speak of." Old Moe looked suddenly sulky and wary. "It may be that something had come innocently into my hands that had been acquired by others in an irregular manner. That's a worry you're always up against in my line of business. The police know it's been an anxiety to me—a great anxiety— for years."

"The police know a good deal more than that." Cadover's glance was now distinctly baleful. "And if Sir John had to put you out of the way of doing mischief for a time, I've no doubt he had good reason. You attacked him, I suppose?"

"Nothing of the sort."

"And it would be with a firearm. You wouldn't be fit for it any other way. It sounds like attempted murder, Steptoe, if you ask me. And there's murder proper in the offing in this case. You know that as well as I do. You've got out of your depth, my man. You've been concerned in the theft of a painting worth tens of thousands of pounds. But now you're much deeper in than that. And now I want the truth out of you. It won't help you much, but it may help a little."

Steptoe, who was now sitting bolt upright on the sofa, gave an uncomfortable wriggle. "There may be something in what you say. But I've been a tool. Business has been bad, sir—very bad indeed. And I was tempted. For no more than fifty pounds, sir. It's painful to think of, I'm sure you'll agree. A respectable trader losing his honour for the promise of a mere

186

fifty quid. I explained all this to your boss. Made a clean breast of it, I did, having seen the error of my ways and being anxious that justice should obtain. And then"—old Moe's voice went quite maudlin with self-pity—"he made this brutal and unprovoked——"

"That will do. We're beginning to get at the truth, and we're not going to go back and waste our time on nonsense. You admit that you have had this stolen painting—the work of an artist called Jan Vermeer of Delft—in your possession?"

There was a short silence. Old Moe looked piteously at Judith, as if hoping that her womanly tenderness might prompt her to some dramatic intervention on his behalf. "Yes—I do."

"Knowing it to be the property of the Duke of Horton?"

"Yes."

"You parted with both that picture, and another known to you to come from the same source, to an artist called Gavin Limbert?"

"I didn't know who he was. He used to come in here from time to time."

"That may be so, Mr Steptoe. But either you, or your associates, subsequently traced Limbert to his studio, and you endeavoured to get the picture back?"

"I put it to him that he'd taken advantage of me, when Gow and Fox were nosing about. It was the sort of dirty trick you might expect an artist to play on you. But this Limbert wasn't an artist, he was a gentleman." Old Moe appeared genuinely aggrieved. "I told him I was surprised at his doing so mean a thing. You'd have felt the same in my place. Particularly with times being so hard for us that's in the luxury trades."

"This afternoon"—Cadover glanced at his watch—

"*yesterday* afternoon you succeeded in abstracting the Vermeer from the premises of a Mr Brown?"

"You can't pin that on me."

"Possibly not. But however that may be, the Vermeer was back here in your shop, and later in the evening Sir John Appleby came to make inquiries about it?"

Old Moe hesitated. He seemed to feel that the point had come at which he must find a line and stick to it. "Sir John certainly did come asking. Pretty well broke in, he did. Must have climbed into my back yard. It isn't legal, that sort of thing—not in this country, it isn't. The Gestapo were the people for——"

"I said we weren't going to listen to nonsense. When Sir John called, were any of your associates here in your shop, or in this office?"

"Certainly not. I was quite alone, which is my habit of an evening."

"You haven't yet told me if you had the picture here."

"Yes, I had."

"Is it here now?"

"It ought to be." Old Moe licked his lips nervously. "If it isn't, you can guess whose fault that is."

"Will you tell me just what you mean by that?"

"Your Sir John Appleby must have made off with it, of course, after nearly murdering me. You've said what a painting like that is worth. Bloody thousands. Even a boss at Scotland Yard would——"

Rather unexpectedly, Cadover broke into a short chuckle. "Come, come, Steptoe. It's an ingenious line, but you know as well as I do that it won't get you anywhere. The Vermeer *is* gone, I take it. Does

188

that mean that some of your friends arrived while Sir John was here?"

"It means what you bloody well care——"

"I won't have that sort of language in Lady Appleby's presence." Almost equally unexpectedly, Cadover was suddenly thunderous. "Whether or not as a result of your contriving to summon them, did your criminal associates arrive and manage to get away with the painting?"

"They came, all right. I got out a telephone message to them. And they'd have a van, and get away with the painting, I suppose."

"What do you mean—you suppose?"

"Because I don't know—see?" Old Moe was stung into a snarl. "When your boss heard my pals down below, he came at me and knocked me out."

"Knocked you right out? You weren't conscious of anything more?"

"Before I fainted away"—old Moe contrived to get much that was piteous into this expression—"I thought I heard him breaking up my shop."

"That's hardly a likely activity, is it? Don't you mean that you heard your friends attacking him?"

"That wouldn't have anything to do with me."

"Wouldn't it?" Cadover was becoming dangerously quiet. "I think you certainly do need that lawyer, Steptoe. And he'll have to begin by painting you a pretty dark picture of your position. But now answer me this. If your friends got away with the Vermeer in that van—which you'll have to describe to me in a minute—just where would they make for?"

"I told you I'm just a tool. My job was to put a ground on the paintings so that they could finally be smuggled away. I was to do that a second time to the

189

Vermeer—after the Vermeer had become a Limbert, as you might say. But they didn't tell me anything about their plans."

"You've no idea of where that van is likely to be now?"

"None whatever."

"Or of where Sir John Appleby is now?"

"I don't know." Steptoe's snarl returned with new violence. "And I couldn't care less."

Judith's heart sank. This part of old Moe's story seemed to her reasonable enough. And she watched Cadover—as if to mark his own sense that here, momentarily, was a dead end—turn and pace to the farther end of the littered and dirty little room.

He had stooped and picked up something from the floor. Now he strode back to Steptoe with an open palm extended before him. "I thought I caught a whiff of powder, Steptoe. And now here's the bullet. Have a look at it."

Steptoe looked sulkily at the small, flattened piece of lead. The sergeant looked at it too. "The light-bulb was shattered, sir, when we entered this room. We had to bring another from downstairs. That would be the shooting, I'd say."

Cadover nodded. "Likely enough. . . . Ugly, isn't it, Steptoe? Brings home to you just what you might be facing."

Old Moe's complexion, which was already an ugly one, took on a yet more displeasing mottle. "It went off in the air," he muttered. "I wasn't going to fire it—just show it by way of defending myself. And then Appleby hit it out of my hand."

"Did Limbert try to hit it out of your hand too—and was he less quick about it?"

"I had nothing to do with that." Steptoe was trembling all over. "None of us had. We talked a lot about how to get the paintings back, but none of us ever thought of that way. We've never committed violence. I swear we haven't."

Cadover pounced. "Then we've got rid of this rubbish about your being an ignorant tool? You've been in on the whole thing—in fact an important member of the gang from the start?"

Steptoe was silent. His eye was still uneasily on the spent bullet.

"Do I understand that, apart from your call on Limbert the day he died, you made no attempt to recover the Vermeer from him until the affair at the Da Vinci yesterday afternoon?"

Steptoe nodded emphatically, and at the same time vigorously sniffed. It looked as if he were preparing to weep. "That's the God's truth, I swear. It took me a long time to trace Limbert at all. And by the next morning he was dead, and there were police all over the place. Then his studio was pretty well sealed up, and we knew we'd have to wait. The trouble was the Stubbs. I'd always said the Stubbs was a mistake. If somebody spotted the Stubbs among Limbert's things, and started asking questions, it would be connected up with what had happened at Scamnum, and the police might think to go over all Limbert's canvases carefully. Otherwise things didn't look too bad. The Vermeer was either still a blank, like I had left it, or Limbert had painted something on it before he died. It didn't look like being worth much more, or being more regarded, the one way or the other. We

191

looked to pick it up when his stuff was sold off—if we didn't have a chance of just clearing out with it earlier."

"It seems we're beginning to get some sense out of you at last." Something almost benevolent had come into Cadover's tone. "As things turned out, how did you know which was the picture you wanted?"

"The dimensions, sir—we knew the dimensions. We had a man of ours giving a hand at the Da Vinci."

"I see. No doubt it was very annoying of this Mr Brown to make a fuss over Limbert's work, and hold a memorial exhibition, and set fancy prices on the things. But why did you risk stealing the picture again yesterday afternoon? Why not just buy it, and avoid piling risk on risk."

"We couldn't afford to."

"That must be nonsense, Inspector." It was Judith who interrupted. "The Da Vinci was probably asking two or three hundred guineas. But these people know quite enough about picture-dealing to realise that they need pay no more than fifty. And it's clear that their resources wouldn't be strained by that."

Cadover nodded and turned to Steptoe. "Well, my man, what have you to say to that?"

"Nothing at all."

"There must have been a reason for your deciding to take a grab at the picture, and not risking attempting to buy. What was it?"

"You know very well what it was, and you've no call to torment me over it." Steptoe at this point evinced what appeared to be a genuine sense of being unfairly treated. "You were on to it, weren't you?"

Cadover, Judith noticed, took a fraction of a second

to consider this. "You felt that the police were on the track of the Vermeer?"

"The chap we'd smuggled into the Da Vinci told us—only yesterday morning, just before the show opened. About somebody snooping round the gallery asking rum questions. And with a camera too, and asking Braunkopf—or Brown, if you like—whether he might photograph the thing." Steptoe paused resentfully. "Probably wanted to dust it for finger-prints as well. That was the bogies, wasn't it? If we hadn't acted quick, they'd have had a report in to your boss, and he'd have sent along and impounded the picture—and in a few days it would have been cleaned up and back at Scamnum. We had to make a grab at it yesterday afternoon, or you and your bogies would have been in on it before us." Steptoe paused again. "Why, this Appleby was there himself making sure of the thing. And we lifted it from under his blood—— from under his bleeding nose. The van was outside and waiting. It was his coming in hot on the trail that gave us the green light to go ahead."

Cadover received this communication with his most wooden face. But Judith was unable to repress a gasp. "You mean to say," she demanded, "that if I hadn't— that if my husband hadn't entered the Da Vinci yesterday afternoon the Vermeer would be there now?"

"It might be. We might have risked waiting a day or two and seeing if we could fix something with Braunkopf. But we couldn't risk that—not with the bogies poking around."

Cadover was looking at his watch. "If by the bogies you mean the police," he said, "you've been barking up the wrong tree." He looked hard at Steptoe. "Do you mean to tell me you don't know there's been another gang after the Vermeer?"

"I don't know what you're talking about."

"Perhaps two other gangs?"

For a moment old Moe's unprepossessing features expressed incredulity and complete bewilderment. Then he gave a gasp of relief. "Hark to him," he said, and looked round as if to command the attention of all in his dingy office. "He's said it, and you're witnesses. The police have reason to believe that a gang of criminals is after that Vermeer. That lets me and my associates out on anything that happened to Limbert. There's been known desperate criminals on the job—quite a different matter from quiet operators on the picture-market like ourselves. Or didn't you say *two* gangs? That's it. Gang warfare. People get killed in that. A shocking thing that the police should be powerless to prevent such outrages. Not English, it isn't. The blood boils." And old Moe, having achieved this brilliant return to form, surveyed Cadover and his subordinates with all the disapproval of an ill-requited tax-payer.

"You're quite right in saying they're a thoroughly desperate lot, Steptoe. Altogether too tough for you and your friends, I can promise you."

"That may well be, sir—that may very well be." Cunning was now discernible as working somewhere in the mind of old Moe. "I was never one for violence, I assure you—nor any of my friends either."

"Would you call them your friends? Haven't they left you rather in the lurch?"

"I was never censorious, sir." Old Moe produced this learned word with a good deal of pride. "I wouldn't blame them for doing the best they can. And

194

I wouldn't go back on them. Not but what"—this afterthought old Moe delivered in some haste—"I wouldn't tell you where they were, if I had any idea of it. For I've seen the error of my ways, and trust my former good character will get me off lightly."

Cadover gave a grunt of disgust. "You certainly hope to get off lightly—with the help of that smart lawyer representing you as what you call a tool. And you hope that your precious friends will get clean away with the Vermeer. And you expect that your fifty pounds—which is much more likely to be five thousand—will be quietly waiting for you somewhere when you come out of prison. Isn't that it? But you're reckoning without your rivals, my friend. If you think they've lost the scent of that picture, you're wrong. Whether two gangs or one, they're hot on top of it now. One lot, if you want to know, is close behind your van at this moment, in a green Humber."

"The green Humber!" Old Moe was startled.

"Means something to you, does it?"

"I saw a green Humber cruising round when I was shutting up the shop. It seemed a bit queer, in a part like this."

"It *was* a bit queer. They'd worked it out that the Vermeer must be back in your possession, Steptoe. And they were waiting for a nice, quiet time of night to break in, cut your throat, and walk off with it. As it was, your friends and their van cut in too early for them. But *not* too early for them to be after it. And when they find a good lonely stretch of road, they'll act. It's likely enough that they've done so by now, and that your confederates are no more than charred corpses in a burnt-out van. . . . You needn't look so

195

scared, man. You're going to be thoroughly safe with us for quite a long time."

Old Moe certainly looked scared; his face showed the sort of terror one might expect to see on a drowning man. Very decidedly, he was now out of his depth. "It's outrageous," he gasped. "Nobody safe . . . the police——"

"The police need information which, as you perfectly well know, you can give them here and now. Withholding it will do you not an atom of good, because your friends are inevitably going to lose that picture. But if you speak up, the judge may regard it as a point in your favour one day. I don't say that he will—I merely mention it as a consideration that may well occur to you."

"What do you want to know?"

"You know very well what I want to know. First, what happened to Sir John Appleby?"

"I've told you—I haven't an idea. He knocked me silly, and then I suppose he went after those friends of mine while they were getting the picture out of my shed. And if they didn't slug him—which mind you they wouldn't do, since we none of us hold with violence—he's probably after them still. Chasing the green Humber in a bleeding Black Maria."

"That's what we have to inquire into. And now, Steptoe—out with it. Where were your friends making for?"

For a moment old Moe was silent. "You're not kidding me about those gangs?" The question had a sudden artlessness that was almost ludicrous.

"No, I'm not. And you saw the green Humber for yourself."

Old Moe nodded, relaxed, and suddenly looked

merely dejected and glum. "A4," he said. "As far as Reading. And then across country to a place north of Fawley on the Berkshire Downs. We decided that in an emergency we must risk trying to fly the picture straight out of the country. There's a man up there with a crate who's willing to take on the job."

Cadover produced his scribbling pad. "I'll just have full directions," he said. "And then you can settle down. You'll be taking it quietly for some time."

12

They were back in the big police car and it was racing through empty London streets. Judith didn't dare to look at her watch, but she knew that it must now be in the small hours. Nor did she want to fire off nervous questions at Cadover. He had done a wonderful job with old Moe. And probably he felt—for he was, Judith knew, a great purist in these matters—that he had skirted the verge of bullying the rascal in order to get the information he had to have. That was an index of his own anxiety about John. So Judith kept her mouth shut.

And presently Cadover spoke. "He must have sailed right in, Lady Appleby."

"I think he must."

"Like him. And I've never known him not come out on top yet."

"I gather he's often been lucky."

"You can call it that. But it's really that he always has in reserve one more punch than they expect. That will be the position at this moment, if you ask me."

It was just what Judith *had* wanted to ask. But she hated questions that were a disguised appeal for emotional reassurance. The car had reached the Embankment and now gathered further speed. There were a few moving lights from craft on Chelsea Reach, and ahead she could hear the long clank and rumble of a freight train crossing the river from Victoria. They turned up Millbank and slowed for a scattering of cars and taxis in Parliament Square. "Late sitting," Judith said mechanically.

Cadover nodded. "When the House rises, they turn off a light on top of the clock tower." He spoke instructively, as if to a child, and Judith knew that he was trying to plan ahead. The car was coming to a halt before he spoke again. "I've got messages out already, I need hardly say. But it will be worth while putting in fifteen minutes organising a better hunt from here. Then I shall go out on that route myself, Lady Appleby, and take over the radio control. This car will take you home. I'll call you up as soon as I hear anything—anything at all." He opened the door and jumped out. "You mustn't worry."

"You've forgotten Mary Arrow." Judith too was out of the car. On either side of her the two great buildings of Scotland Yard—penny-plain and twopence-coloured—were like the walls of a canyon.

"I'm trying not to forget anything." Cadover had a moment to spare for mild irony.

"I'm sorry. I mean, you've forgotten it was agreed that I should go to her. May I come in?"

"We'll go and find her—almost first thing. This door, please."

Uniformed men were handing Cadover messages

almost before he stepped across the threshold. Some he received in silence; others elicited curt orders; and meanwhile he was striding up a long corridor. Judith followed. The place was unfamiliar at this hour. There was a smell of soap and water; she glanced down a side corridor and saw a squad of men at work with buckets and mops. So that's how it's done, she thought. It would be useful in the home. But noisy.... Her stomach gave a jump and she realised that she was moving upwards in a lift.

She knew Cadover's room, having once or twice been received in it with some ceremony. But for a moment it seemed wholly strange. Bleak, untinted fluorescent lighting flooded it, and made the four or five persons present look like so many animated corpses. The largest wall, commonly embellished with a scatter of current police notices headed *Lost* or *Wanted for Murder* or *£100 Reward* cheek by jowl with signed photographs of departed Home Secretaries, had disappeared behind an enormous map. Before the map was a long table with a battery of telephones. Now on one and now on another of these a red light glowed. Three constables were receiving and jotting down messages. Receiving these at a desk was a young man with a public-school face, keyed-up and nervous, who read them and at the same time talked continuously into a microphone. It was not spectacular, but Judith judged that its efficiency was deadly. When battles are being fought, she thought, there are always places like this. And always with that young man. John, she supposed, must have begun like that.... She found a chair and sat down. A ship's siren wailed, far down the river. And, just outside, some one went past with a clanking pail and mop.

Cadover spent what must have been ten minutes without taking his eyes from the big map. He appeared to be laying down the broad lines of some proposed operation to another detective-inspector who stood beside him making an occasional note. Judith knew that it would be useless to attempt to follow this. She was excited and she was anxious. But she was also tired out, so that she wondered how long she could sit unregarded here without slipping off to sleep. It wasn't much of a chair; if she did doze off, she would probably come down with a bump. And that wouldn't do at all. . . . She raised her head with a jerk, and saw that Cadover was approaching her. She jumped up. And although she had resolved to ask no questions she found herself saying, "Is there any news?"

He shook his head. "Nothing yet."

"I hardly expected anything—yet."

"We make a bit of progress—in a negative way. But there's only one certainty so far."

"About——?"

"About the Vermeer, Lady Appleby—about the Vermeer. It won't leave these islands by air to-night." He was suddenly impatient. "Steptoe's friends must be fools to think of such a thing."

"And the other gangs—do you think they are fools too?"

He looked at her sharply. "They're uncommonly foolishly employed. I wonder if that's the only reason why there's a lot in the affair that just doesn't make sense."

"You find it like that?" Judith felt some diffidence in advancing an opinion to this sombre professional.

202

"It seemed to me to be coming together, more or less."

"It has to come together *in toto*, Lady Appleby, before we can take much satisfaction in sitting back and looking at it. Didn't one of the men you overheard—Zhitkov—say that Steptoe had been the unknown factor in his scheme . . . something like that?"

"Yes, I'm quite confident he said it in almost exactly those words."

"Quite so. And don't both Zhitkov and Cherry appear to have been unknown factors in Steptoe's scheme? Wouldn't you agree that he really did know something about them?"

"It certainly looked like that."

"Well, if *we* can be said to have a scheme, I suspect there's an unknown factor in that too."

"Perhaps by this time it's not unknown to John."

Cadover stared at her. Then—to the general surprise of the room—he laughed aloud. "Capital," he said. "That's the most sensible idea I've heard tonight. And now we'll go and see Miss Arrow. She's just along the corridor. A good deal better, too, according to the doctor."

Judith was dismayed. "You're not going to try to make the poor woman talk?"

"I think she may want to talk. I'm sure I hope so."

"You think it might be important?"

"I have an idea—less rational than I commonly go in for, Lady Appleby—that she holds the key to the whole thing."

The police surgeon was quite young—little older than the man who had talked into the microphone at the desk. Judith rather doubted the possibility of his possessing that store of experience with which Cadover had credited him. But he appeared to take the case of Mary Arrow in his stride. "Undoubtedly a genuine instance of total amnesia, Inspector." He turned to Judith. "Loss of memory, that is to say."

Judith received this doubtless well-meant effort at education stonily. It was rather cool, she was thinking, carrying off a sick woman to a glorified police-station. She ought to have been put in an ambulance and taken to one of the big hospitals. But then somebody had to have the habit of being cool, and keeping cool—on a night like this. . . . "Where is she?" she asked.

"In the next room. We'll go in as soon as I've told the Inspector what I can. Are you a relative?"

"This is Lady Appleby." Cadover was scandalised. "How is Miss Arrow's memory now?"

"The amnesic state began to break up only a few hours ago. When somebody found her——"

Judith interrupted. "I found her, Doctor."

"I see. Well, I've no doubt you concluded she was in a very confused condition. In many cases that lasts for quite a time. But this woman is getting things sorted out rather remarkably. She's very clear about the place and time at which things began coming back to her. Victoria Station at midnight. She felt dazed, but her only real surprise was at the lateness of the hour. So she went home, and made some tea, and talked to somebody. That would be you, Lady Appleby?"

"Yes."

"When I first saw her, less than an hour ago, she was worrying over never having known anybody called Judith. She was hiding behind that fictitious worry, you might say, from what is her real trouble. It was her last attempt at dodging. But she's out in the open now. Shall we go in, Inspector?"

"Just one moment." Cadover paused by the next door. "Miss Arrow has been dodging in more senses than one. We've been looking for her for over a week, without coming upon as much as a trace. Total amnesia may be common enough, but that sort of successful disappearance with it is not. Have you gathered anything that might explain it?"

"She says that at Victoria she was puzzled by another thing. She had hardly any money in her purse. And she was puzzled about *why* she was puzzled, because in point of fact she never does carry about very much. What she does do is to keep ten pounds or so in cash in her flat, against emergencies. So she'd probably set out in the first instance with that."

Cadover nodded. "Quite right. It fits in with what I know. By the way, did she have a tooth-brush on her?"

The young police-surgeon stared. "As a matter of fact, there's a tooth-brush in her bag. I noticed it when she took out a powder compact. Talking of that sort of thing, by the way, she's quite clean. Baths, I'd say."

Judith compressed her lips. At any moment one might be knocked down by a bus, and instantly one would be treated not as a person but a thing. . . . Involuntarily she asked, "Why *not* baths?"

"The point, Lady Appleby, is that Miss Arrow didn't go careless about that sort of ordinary routine. And that means that she probably didn't, in any very immediately obvious way, go helpless either. And that in turn means that she could probably so plan, and so conduct herself, as to avoid discovery by her relations or by the police. She's been in hiding, in every sense. That's the whole idea, I need hardly say, of any form of hysterical fugue." The police-surgeon opened the door. "Most of them fail at it, almost at once—so far as successful physical flight goes. Behave in a lost or *outré* fashion, and are picked up and lodged in hospital before they can say Jack Robinson. . . . Well, Miss Arrow"—and the young man's voice took on a briskly professional cheerfulness and confidence—"here are some friends of yours. . . . Drunk up your coffee? That's splendid."

"They make wonderful coffee here. Nobody could resist it, Doctor."

If a capacity for polite mockery was an index of mental balance, Judith thought, then Mary Arrow was indeed securely on her pins again. Physically, however, she still seemed worn out; her grey jersey was not more devoid of colour than her complexion, and the shadows under her eyes were still as black as her slacks. Lying back in a deep arm-chair, she glanced from one of her visitors to another. Then she gave a faint smile. "The unknown Judith."

Judith went over to her. "Are you reasonably comfortable, Mary?"

"It wouldn't be very polite to say otherwise. Didn't you tell me your husband ran part of this place? I've been looking forward to meeting him."

"John is—not here at the moment."

"Pity." Mary seemed to have lost interest. She put both her feet flat on the floor, as if to test what weight they might be able to carry. "I think I'll go home now."

Judith felt Cadover stiffen beside her. He took a step forward. "There is a car waiting, Miss Arrow,

206

to take you where you wish to go at any time. Only——"

"It's something to learn that. I was beginning to think that perhaps I was detained—isn't that the word?"

"Nobody can be detained, except in the imagination of journalists." The purist in Cadover had risen up. "You are perfectly free to leave at any time. Only, sooner or later, you must tell us anything you can that may shed light on the death of Mr Limbert. I fully realise the very distressing——"

"No more professional touch, Inspector—please. I've had a stiff dose of it on the medical side." Mary Arrow frowned. "I'm still behaving pretty oddly, I suppose? There seems no call for me to be rude. And of course I'll tell you what I can. But I'd rather it wasn't to-night. There are things about it that make it rather a strain to face up to. After all, that's why I and my wits together cleared out as they did. That—and being slugged on the head."

"Slugged on the head!" Cadover turned to the surgeon. "Is there any——"

"There's some indication of a fall or a blow." The young man was cautious. "And if Miss Arrow suffered both a nervous trauma and a physical injury, that would go a long way to explain——"

"No doubt." Cadover was regarding Mary Arrow with frank anxiety—and it was the first time, Judith reflected, that she had seen that expression plainly on his face.

Mary had managed to get to her feet. "To-morrow," she said. "To-morrow—if you like."

"I don't want to press you in any way. But there are circumstances making it very important that I should get all the information I can, here and now."

"Gavin is dead. That's the only terribly important circumstance I know, I'm afraid. But come to-morrow. Or I'll come back here." She turned to Judith. "Will your husband be in then? I've an idea he's the person I'd like to explain things to."

Judith shook her head—and tried to keep all anxiety out of her voice. "I'm afraid I can't tell wheth-er——"

But Cadover was less scrupulous. "Miss Arrow, please listen to me carefully. It would be Lady Appleby's husband who would be questioning you now, were he here in his Department. But he isn't. And we none of us know where he is. But we do know that it is his concern with Gavin Limbert's death that has taken him away. It begins to look—and I don't try to disguise this from Lady Appleby—as if it had taken him into danger. That's sometimes our trade here, and his trade's a thing that Sir John is uncommonly fond of. If we are to back him up, we must have the fullest picture we can get."

Mary had sat down again. She was looking at Cadover with rounded eyes. "And what I can remember might help?"

"Certainly. There is some piece of confused and desperate mischief going on somewhere at this moment, and it is bound up in some way we don't understand with Limbert's death. Sir John may be in the thick of it."

Mary frowned. It was as if she still had some difficulty in sorting out the reports of the world actually about her. Then she put out a hand and touched Judith's. "I didn't understand," she said. "You'll think me heartless—downright low. But I thought all this

208

was only academic. The Law, and Punishment, and Protecting Society. I had no idea . . . about your husband." She turned back to Cadover. "For goodness sake get it all out of me quick."

The young surgeon had gone. In his place there had appeared a sergeant who was preparing to take shorthand notes. He was an elderly man, compounded of fatherliness and discretion. And Cadover, who himself carried round with him permanently something of the same character, had positively disposed his features, Judith believed, in enhanced lines of wise benevolence. It was a place in which they all worked very hard, she thought. And, certainly, nobody worked harder than John. But his interest in *this* affair had been of her own making. If she hadn't led him that dance to the Da Vinci——

Judith realised that for some moments she had lost herself in reverie. *The events of the night of Monday the twenty-second.* She was not sure whether it was Cadover or the sergeant who had given this out as a sort of text for the inquiry that was opening. *A private view.* Mary would have to tell them about that. *The events of the night of Monday the twenty-second began with a private view. A private view of what, madam? Of Lady Clancarron emptying out the baby with the bath water. And you have a photograph of this destructive proceeding? No, sir—but I have a pleasing snap of The Fifth and Sixth Days of Creation. . . .*

Judith jerked herself awake. A drift of chill night air from the uncurtained window by which she was sitting made her shiver. An oblong of darkness now, it looked by day across the river to the County Hall, backed by the smoke of Waterloo. She had a sudden sense of the immensity of London, stretching round her in unending reticulations slashed through by the black and winding river. Deep below her feet was the empty Underground; above her head, in further bleak and functional rooms, other C.I.D. men sat up late over other murders, disappearances, robberies, treasons, thefts. And all around the pausing city was the further darkness of nocturnal England, stained with the dull glow of sleeping towns, shot with the glare of foundries, probed by the innumerable headlights of heavy night-travelling lorries with their burden of bricks, of car-bodies, of cement, of the family possessions of clerks, artisans, school-teachers following the drift of labour. And among them was a van carrying— fantastically—Vermeer's Aquarium. A dark van, hurtling through the English darkness, and containing that other and unearthly darkness of a submarine world in which a dozen grotesquely imagined monsters, large and small, miraculously generated their own conflicting systems of jewelled and coloured light. How had the painter of the tranquil town, the little street, the daughter in fancy-dress, the lace-maker over her bobbins, come to imagine this remote universe, which only the modern bathysphere had vindicated as true? Nobody could tell. And nobody might ever see that picture again. Or John Appleby again. . . .

Judith took herself in hand and listened. *The events of the night of Monday the twenty-second.* Mary was talking—coherently, and only occasionally prompted by a question from Cadover.

"He had gone over to the Thomas Carlyle. Not that he was a member; he thought the place absurd and squalid, and he had no business there at all. Only he said it sometimes gave him ideas. It seems that an abstract painter is as dependent as any other on keeping an eye on things and people around him. Gavin claimed that he had a right to drop in on the club just in a neighbourly way. And nobody ever stopped him. He usually managed to please himself, you see. He was forceful—and at the same time he had a great deal of what, I suppose, is called charm. . . . I used to think it would bring him trouble one day. It would be so desolating a thing to find himself possessed of, if ever he found that he possessed nothing else—nothing, I mean, of what he hoped and dreamed of. I never deluded myself into thinking that, if his talent betrayed him, he would think anything of possessing me.

"He had been to the club—just a look-in, quite early—and when he got back—it must have been before midnight—he came up to talk to me. He talked——"

"Up by the fire-escape, Miss Arrow?"

"No—the ordinary inside staircase. He talked for quite a long while. Sometimes he seemed to wind himself up for work in that way—by . . . by just talking, and then going straight down to work. He had met an old school-fellow who had shared his interest in painting—somebody called Crabbe, who had looked, Gavin said, pretty down and out. He said I might meet this Crabbe some time, because he had given him an invitation to drop in. He talked about other things too. Would you want to hear them?"

"Anything about a man called Steptoe?"

"Yes." Mary looked surprised. "I'd never heard of this Steptoe before, but Gavin made him sound ex-

211

tremely amusing. He had bought an old canvas from Steptoe, and also a junk-shop painting about which he was very excited, because he was convinced it was by George Stubbs. Well, this man had turned up on him that day and tried to buy the things back. Gavin said it made him feel suspicious; that possibly the Stubbs *was* a real Stubbs, and stolen property, so that perhaps he ought to tell the police. I don't think he said more about Steptoe than that."

"Did he, either at this or any other time, mention to you somebody called Cherry?"

"I'm sure he didn't."

"You know Zhitkov, Miss Arrow—the sculptor on your ground floor? Was Mr Limbert on terms of any special intimacy with him? Did he ever do business with him in any way?"

"I don't think so. I doubt whether they ever did much more than pass the time of day."

"And he didn't mention Zhitkov to you in any connection on this occasion?"

"I don't think so. But—wait—yes, he did. He said something about Crabbe's having said something about Zhitkov. I think Crabbe had asked him if he'd seen Zhitkov that evening, or if Zhitkov was about— something like that. It was a bare mention. Gavin put no emphasis on it."

"Thank you. And then——" Cadover checked himself at a knock upon the door. A constable came in and handed him a message. He glanced at it, dismissed the man, read the message more carefully, seemed about to say something prompted by it, and then changed his mind. "And this takes us past midnight, Miss Arrow?"

"Long past it. I used to forget about time when

Gavin and I were talking. It must seem absurd, but I've really no idea of how long Gavin stayed. When eventually he went away, he started off by the inside staircase. But he was hardly out of the door before he was back again. 'People prowling,' he said—or something like that."

"Wasn't that rather strange, at such an hour?"

"Well, people do come rather oddly in from time to time. A drunk sleeps on a landing, or a couple make love on the stairs. Studio folk are known to be tolerant about such things. I didn't think anything of it at the time. You see, Gavin loved his little conspiratorial route by the fire-escape, and I thought he was just saying the first thing that came into his head, in order to have the fun of playing that game. Anyway, he went off down the escape, and I closed my window after him. It was high time to go to bed. I was just beginning to get undressed when I heard a bang. Gavin always closed his shutters at night, and I thought the sound must have been his doing that, for some reason extra hard. But somewhere in my mind I must have known it was nothing of the sort. I found myself restless and anxious. But I told myself I was being a fool; that it was only because we hadn't made love."

The sergeant's pencil travelled smoothly over his pad. Cadover appeared to be studying his own toes. For Judith an almost unbearable suspense was building up, and she was unable to take her eyes for a moment from Mary's face.

"I remembered what Gavin had said about prowlers. But some time had passed before that. I'd tried to read a book. When I did remember, I opened the door of my flat and took a cautious look downstairs. I could just make out two or three figures on Gavin's

213

landing. They were whispering—purposeful whispering, not any sort of whispering one might expect. I caught some sentences. One of them said, 'It's a raid on that club—nothing more than that. And they'll be clearing off any time now.' And another said, 'It would be quieter with a key, all the same; perhaps there's one in the room of the other fellow downstairs.' I couldn't make it out, but I was very frightened. I went back into the flat and shut the door."

Mary paused. Cadover too was now absorbed. His heavy breathing could be heard in the silence. What must have been a lorry piled with empty milk cans rattled over Westminster Bridge.

"And then I went down the fire-escape. Gavin's shutters were closed—and bolted too. There was nothing out-of-the-way in that. I used to knock if I wanted to get in. The lights were on inside. You can see through, because there are two of those little diamond-shaped holes. I've told Lady Appleby how we made a game of them; about—about my private view."

There was another silence. For the first time, Mary seemed to have difficulty in continuing. Cadover looked up. "And what did you see, Miss Arrow, on the occasion in question?" The official phrase fell with well-calculated gravity and impersonality upon the room.

"Gavin seemed to be working. That was what I'd have expected, and for a moment I was relieved. He often worked at drawing right through the night. And he had spoken of making a start at blocking out something on his new canvas."

Cadover looked up sharply. "You mean the canvas he'd had from Steptoe? And he'd spoken of making a

214

start on it? He hadn't done anything on it so far?"

"It had certainly been a blank that morning. I couldn't properly see what was happening, because the easel seemed to have been moved from its usual place. But presently I did catch a glimpse of something that surprised me. The man at the easel wasn't drawing. He was painting in oils. And in that instant I *knew*. . . . It was like a physical blow, and I must have cried out. The man at the easel thrust away his palette and whirled round towards the window. Of course it wasn't Gavin. It was somebody I'd never seen before—a man with a twisted lip."

This time the silence seemed very long. Cadover sat fixed in thought. Mary Arrow's eyes were unnaturally dilated; she must, Judith guessed, be re-living her experience in terms of sheer hallucination. When at length she spoke again it was very quietly.

"And my cry was fatal to him. He was caught completely off his guard. There was a click at the door, and men in the room. The man dived for something— I don't know what—and in the same instant there was just such another bang as I had heard before. This time, I knew what it was. The man who had been pretending to be a painter absorbed in his work dropped out of my field of vision. But I was certain he was dead.

"I think there were three men. I couldn't see much, and it was difficult to count. They seemed to be behaving like madmen who were bent on destroying everything they could lay their hands on."

"They were searching the studio, were they not?"

"It must have been that. I started to batter at the shutters. And at that moment the thing happened—

215

the thing that pretty well finished me for the time. Two of them had pitched aside a sofa that was in their way. It just went past my field of view. And then they pitched aside something else. But that fell full on the patch of floor that I could clearly see. It was Gavin with the top of his head blown off."

"Miss Arrow, you needn't tell us more." Cadover had got to his feet and was making an odd, compassionate gesture. He was clearly deeply distressed. "I can only say——"

"Let me go on. There's hardly anything more that I can tell. Perhaps more of my memory will come back later. Now, there's no more of it that is—is consecutive. There may have been an interval while I did a faint—something like that. Certainly I got back to my room and out on the staircase. The men had come out of Gavin's studio and let the door lock itself behind them. I saw Zhitkov's door open and some sort of flurry there. I thought I heard a groan. Then I realised that they were bundling a body down the stairs— bundling it down as if it were a sack. I thought it was Gavin's and I flew at them. I remember somebody turning and looking surprised. Perhaps he hit me. After that there is just nothing at all. Except that I can see a sort of picture of myself, staggering upstairs to fetch something—something that I must have in order to follow I didn't know what."

"Money." Cadover spoke very gently. "Money, Miss Arrow—and a tooth-brush."

13

"Slough, Maidenhead, Twyford." The great car was moving like a projectile, but Cadover from the darkness spoke as if his eyes were still fixed on the map in his room now far behind them. "They can't have made any great speed. Any minute we may hear from Reading that it's all over. Some excellent people in Reading."

Judith leant forward to peer at the speedometer. The dashboard showed a multiplicity of illuminated disks, large and small; it was like a model of the planets and their satellites in an up-to-date museum. Or you might fancy you were in an air-liner in the stratosphere. The car travelled as smoothly as that. It was a good road.

Her eye found the right instrument just as the green light behind it changed to red. That might be to suggest, perhaps, that mild hazard attached to such a speed through the night. The needle stood without a tremor at eighty. In an uncanny way the straight rib-

217

bon of macadam fed itself into the devouring car. It was like being one of those gadgets holding a tape-measure that whips itself out of sight on the pressing of a button. . . . How idiotically, Judith thought, the mind behaves in a state of tension—hunting similes like a jaded novelist. It would be better if she could talk. But the car was full of voices, an orderly succession of voices issuing from the darkness just below the extended constellation of glowing instruments. For the most part Cadover just listened to the voices, but sometimes he conversed with them. It was like some queer *séance* in which a host of well-drilled spirits had been taught to wait their turn. . . . There— she was at it again.

"It sounds like a funeral." Judith realised that the voices had been faded out; that Cadover was speaking to her; and that he too had produced a simile.

"Like a funeral, Inspector?"

"Only in a manner of speaking." Cadover seemed to feel that his association of ideas had been a little unfortunate. "An oddly-assorted group of vehicles, going along at rather a slow pace. It was that, you see, that caught the eye of a constable outside Slough, and brought us in our first report."

"Of the van? I'm afraid I've got a bit confused about all this."

"What he first noticed was the old Baby Austin. Runs one himself, maybe. In front of that was the motor-cycle, and in front of that again the green Humber saloon."

"And the van?"

"It was there, all right, and at first he supposed it was holding up everything behind it. But there was a clear road, and he suddenly had the idea that here

218

was a sort of procession. And so, of course, it was—
as we very well know. Smart man, it seems. What he
saw was very trivial—but slightly odd, all the same.
So he took the number of the Austin, which was the
only one left in view. When he got back to his station,
and was questioned as a result of my message having
been received there, of course he remembered all
this at once."

"But the Austin——" Judith checked herself. The
voices had begun again. It was some minutes before
she was able to say, "But the Austin would make one
too many?"

"It's presence at the tail of the procession may have
been accidental, of course. But it was still there at
Maidenhead, and naturally we're taking no chances.
It's being traced now."

"Traced?" Judith frowned into the darkness.
"Surely we're tracing the whole lot."

"Not the Austin itself, but its registration." Cadover
was completely patient. "Name of the owner. You
never can tell."

"I see." Judith felt stupid and exhausted. "You'd
better not bother to go on explaining, Inspector. I
don't want to be a blight."

Cadover took her hand and pressed it. It was one
of his unexpected moments. "You'll be better, Lady
Appleby, keeping your mind on it and knowing what's
what. It seems there's a lot of army stuff on the move
to-night, and the contact near Maidenhead was a result of that. Our procession seems to have got mixed
up with a line of tanks on carriers, and a military patrol
on a motor-cycle had the job of feeding it out. By that
time the order had changed. First the van, then the

Austin, then the Humber, and the motor-cyclist last of all."

"You get all this over your radio?"

"Certainly. Of course, we've had a bit of luck. It was only ten minutes ago that one of our men came up with the army fellow and made the contact. And the news from Twyford has been luck too. An R.A.C. patrol getting home late after a break-down. The procession had passed him, head on, not ten minutes before our people questioned him. By this time it was the van, the Humber, the motor-cycle. Either he didn't see the Austin, or it wasn't there. So it does look as if we can count the Austin out. And now we should hear from Reading at any moment. I never expected to get a net round the thing as close in as that."

"Reading isn't our last chance?"

"You might call it our last chance of a quick, neat job. Steptoe spoke about a place on the Downs north of Fawley, but I haven't great faith in the van's really making for there once the folk in it are really alarmed. Too much chance of being met at their destination by something uncomfortable. After all, they must have known that old Moe was booked for gaol, and they're not likely to have great faith in his keeping his mouth shut. So my reading of their minds is this: they'll be arguing and wondering—and already they'll be a good deal worried by that Humber. While that's going on, they'll stick rather half-heartedly to the route as planned, and to the idea of a rendezvous with the fellow who has a plane waiting. But eventually fright will gain the upper hand with them, and they'll try simply going to earth in whatever rural seclusion they

220

can find. I want to get them before that stage. . . .
Ah—that must be Reading."

Cadover bent down and flicked a switch. Judith's
ear, unaccustomed to short-wave transmission, caught
only a word here and there. Again Cadover flicked
the switch, and there was silence. "Not Reading, after
all?" she asked.

"Not Reading. The Yard. The Austin is registered
in the name of Hildebert Braunkopf or Brown."

This news was bewildering; the news that presently
came in from Reading was bad. Its tenor was simple:
the whole procession as it now was—van, Humber,
and motor-cycle—had got clean away and disappeared. Of how this came about, Judith formed no
clear picture at the time. She was aware, indeed, of
only one urgent and shattering fact. The news in-
cluded news of John. And this she could only think
of as bad news too.

The van—she was later to understand—had been
spotted as it approached the town, and the police were
prepared for it. At the first point where the road ran
between solid walls a simple road-block had been got
ready. A lorry was to be driven sharply out of a yard
as the van approached. The whole procession would
thus be obliged to draw up, and a strong force of police
would immediately converge upon it from the surrounding buildings and from the rear. What was to
make this plan unsuccessful was fright—that very
fright which Cadover had predicted would at some
point overtake the men in the van. Possibly they had
become aware of the police. More probably, it was
the pursuing Humber that had got them down. In the
outskirts of the town they had suddenly crammed on

221

speed. To get clear of the Humber in open country would of course have been impossible; it was by far the faster vehicle. The idea of the driver of the van, as he jammed his accelerator down, must have been to gain a momentary lead, and then to give his pursuer the slip by plunging into the side-streets of the town. But the result was unforeseen and dramatic. Suddenly confronted by an improvised cul-de-sac, the driver of the van had braked, skidded, lost all control of his vehicle, blindly accelerated again, and driven straight into a brick wall. Or rather he had driven straight *through* a brick wall, across a yard, and over a decayed wooded fence into a lane at the back. And what the van had achieved by chance the Humber immediately achieved by brilliant driving—so that both vehicles vanished, leaving the police standing. And meanwhile the motor-cyclist, sufficiently far behind to avoid capture from the rear, had turned tail and himself achieved a successful get-away.

But if the police had thus, for the time, failed in their design, there was one individual, it appeared, who was not inappreciative of their efforts. A single constable, pounding heroically on foot in pursuit of the disappearing vehicles, had come, far up the lane, upon a small bundle of flaming wood-wool. Attached to this ingenious signal by the length of two shoe-laces was a scrap of official paper. And on this there had been hastily scrawled:

> *Well tried, Reading. Keep it up.*
> *J. Appleby*
> Ass'. Comm'.

"So that's all right." It was Cadover who was addressing her. The message lay between them on a bare scrubbed table. Cadover had all the appearance of a sudden access of well-founded confidence. Judith wondered if it could possibly be genuine. She had seen Cadover play-acting for the benefit of others; it seemed likely that he was only putting on an encouraging turn now.

"All right?" Judith looked about her. The pursuit had demonstrably come to a stop; the hurtling car had been exchanged for this bleak little police-station she didn't know where; through an open door she could see some sort of mobile radio in a huge van, and men standing by with motor-cycles waiting for messages that didn't come. "Really—all right?" She looked at the message again. "He must be in the van—a prisoner."

"He may be the one without being the other." Cadover turned aside to give orders. He was as brisk as he had been hours before—Judith found she couldn't reckon how many hours before. The map of southern England which had covered the wall of his room at Scotland Yard now appeared to be lodged firmly within his head. He rapped out road-numbers, mileages, junctions to men who came and went unceasingly in the little room. Listening to him quartering the countryside, Judith knew very well that he would come out on top; that his quarry could not possibly escape him. His grasp was too sure, and the ultimate size of his battalions too big, for that. And perhaps he meant no more than this when he said that it was all right. Experimentally she said, "John will be all right?"

"He'll be all right now—and, mind you, I thought

he might have had his throat cut." Cadover contrived a very good care-free chuckle.

"But if he's in the hands of those people——"

"They know that, ten to one, their little game is up. That *all* their little games are up. And that's likely to make them quite respectful. They're not homicidal maniacs, you know."

"They killed——" Judith checked herself. "I suppose it's pretty well a matter of waiting for daylight?"

Cadover nodded. "That's likely enough. Only, I've some hopes of the telephone."

"The telephone—you're expecting a message?"

"Not exactly that. The point is that this pursuit must be mainly of subordinates. The van itself may have the boss of one lot—Steptoe's lot. But the Humber seems to contain only henchmen of Zhitkov's, and the man on the motor-cycle is presumably just some one ordered about by Cherry. If the men in the van manage to give their pursuers the slip for a bit, they may very well try to contact Steptoe, by way of discovering whether we've picked him up or not. And the other fellows, if they get a bit foxed, are likely to ring up their respective bosses for instructions."

"Cherry and Zhitkov? They went off together."

"Quite so. And a call that gets the one may get the other—supposing, that is, they're still as thick as thieves." Cadover found time to treat this sally as a joke of some magnitude. "Crooks often don't realise how much one can do with the telephone-people giving one a hand." Cadover went to the door, fired off a rapid round of instructions, and then came back. "But we may have to wait for morning, all the same. . . . Ah—coffee."

A rural constable had come in with steaming enamel

224

mugs. Judith accepted hers gratefully. Perhaps, after all, Mary Arrow had been serious when she commended the similar coffee served at Scotland Yard. The hot, sweet stuff quickened her blood as if it were a powerful drug. She looked at her watch. Four o'clock. It wasn't much more than twelve hours since all this had begun—begun with a freakish visit to the gallery of the mysterious Hildebert Braunkopf. For mysterious he had now become. According to any feasible interpretation of the affair, he ought by now to have withdrawn unobtrusively into the wings, with no chance of a final bow before the curtain. Or he ought to be tucked up snugly in bed, with—or rather, like—Grace Brooks and Lady Clancarron. Instead of which, he was at large in a Baby Austin. . . .

Judith dozed uneasily. From a burning house—Shelley's father-in-law had maintained—it would be incumbent upon one to drag the philosopher Fénelon before the philosopher Fénelon's pretty maid-servant. Or—Godwin had added—before one's own mother, either. But what if John and Vermeer's Aquarium were in the same burning van? She would haul out John. But suppose the human being was old Moe? And suppose it wasn't just one Vermeer but all the Vermeers—and all the El Grecos and all the Rembrandts too? Judith jerked herself awake and looked at her watch again. One minute past four. At this rate it would never be five o'clock; first there would be the end of the world. They used to call that the Great Combustion. . . . Again she had a vivid mental picture of a blazing van. She heard the crackle of the flames, opened her eyes, and realised that she was listening to some operational noise from the radio. A car engine started up, then a motor-cycle, then several more cars. Somebody was giving a quick succession of orders, she heard more engines far away, the whole place was in a bustle. And the light was different. She looked a third time at her watch. It was ten minutes to six. Cadover stood before her. She had the impression—but that, surely, must be a delusion—that he simply picked her up and threw her into a car.

Certainly she was in a car, and it was moving. But this time the very pulse of the engine sounded different. It might have been some great hunting animal that had lain baffled all night in a thicket, and now knew itself to be moving in to the kill.

"I sent a message to Scamnum for the Duke." Cadover was now clearly visible beside Judith. "He must be a bit anxious about his property, poor old chap."

That, thought Judith, was one way of looking at it. Aloud, she said, "It was the telephone—that got us moving?"

"Yes—a couple of hours ago, and from a call-box pretty well where we expected it. Of course one can't be sure. It's a matter of interpreting a few sentences. But I'm pretty confident it was the man on the motorcycle—Cherry's man—calling up reinforcements from some place near Uxbridge. It might be where Cherry and Zhitkov went off to, and now they may be making for the scene themselves. The place in Uxbridge is being investigated now. . . . Pleasant open country here."

Judith looked about her in a grey dawn. The new journey seemed to be going on for a long time. She no longer had any clear idea about what part of England this was. They were moving through a broad prospect of bare fields which here and there sloped down into valleys still shrouded in mist—and over the brown fields themselves drifts of vapour were eddying and dissolving one by one, like the last belated dancers at a ball. The hedging and ditching was good, she thought inconsequently; it was well-cared-for country. A thick dark barrier of thorn whipped past almost under her nose, for they had left the main roads far behind them, and this was little more than a lane. But still the car was travelling very fast; she twisted her head and saw that it had outdistanced the line of four or five purposeful police-vehicles in the rear. The scale of the affair had become fantastic—it was queer that all this commotion should be caused by a quiet Dutch painter who had died nearly three hundred years ago.

Cadover talked over his radio. In daylight the process seemed altogether less mysterious. As the car swung round a corner he sat back with an air of finality. "Got them," he said.

"You really know?"

"Yes. The first report was from a local man, and I couldn't be sure. But I have one fellow of my own out ahead, and there's no doubt about it. Dark furniture van, green Humber, another big car." He pointed straight ahead, over the driver's shoulder. "See that hill?"

"Yes." The hill was quite a landmark—a first bold sweep of downland, announcing a change in the character of the terrain beyond. "They're up there?" There was mist on the summit still. But even as she looked, this began to lift like a slow curtain.

Cadover had a map open on his knee. "Look near the brow, on our left," he said. "There—where the mist's just rising. You see a scar?"

"It looks like a stone-quarry."

"That's what it is—an abandoned one. The van has gone to earth there. And the other fellows have found it out."

Judith's heart beat faster. "You mean there's a sort of siege?"

"That's about the size of it. In the middle of an English countryside. They must be crazy." Cadover sounded disgusted. "Haven't stopped to consider that the police may be right on top of them. It's sheer desperation."

"You think they might fight?"

"Among themselves, Lady Appleby? It wouldn't surprise me if they were occupied that way now."

"And fight the police as well?"

"They won't do *that* for long." Cadover's voice was grim. "One doesn't get worked up about thieves and burglars in a general way. But this sort of outrage——" He checked himself. "Listen."

Judith found that she was trembling. "It wouldn't just be quarrymen blasting—something like that?"

Cadover made no reply to this futile question. He was talking into his machine. Then he leant forward and spoke to the driver. The car braked swiftly and came to a stop. Cadover opened a door. "Will you jump out?" he said.

Judith jumped out. "Are we——"

Cadover had dexterously closed the door again. He spoke to her through the open window. "I'm sorry, Lady Appleby—but I'm going in first. And you'll be better a bit behind. The last car will pick you up."

"You can't possibly——"

"I couldn't take the responsibility, ma'am. . . . Drive ahead."

And Cadover's car leapt forward. She was left in a cloud of dust.

It had happened so rapidly that for some seconds Judith was merely bewildered. Then she was furious—and not the less so because her fury had to be directed against the universe at large. It would be unfair to blame Cadover; she had no business being in this chase at all; not a plurality of husbands incarcerated by criminals in sinister vans would give her the faintest title to go charging about in cars from Scotland Yard. Cadover had no doubt been uneasy about her from the start; she was as anomalous to his purism—as ectopic, that was the word—as the blondes in the bomb-racks of an American war film. . . . His car was now far ahead, sweeping round in a broad circle that climbed at an easy gradient up the hill. She could just hear another car approaching behind her. There would be several more behind that. And the very last and dustiest had been instructed to pick her up. It was probably a mobile canteen, stuffed with the disgusting objects called hot-dogs and spouting atrocious coffee at every chink. And Judith's pride revolted. She would *not* be turned into a camp-follower—a *vivandière* of the constabulary. . . . She found herself staring at a small sign-post, and felt like picking up a stone and having a shy at it. Then she saw that it said *Public Footpath*, and that it pointed straight up the hill.

In an instant she was over the stile to which the signpost pointed, and as she dropped to the ground she heard the second car go past. Before her, the path skirted a couple of ploughed fields and then ran over turf directly to the summit. It looked as if it must pass close to the lip of the quarry. And Judith ran. She couldn't beat Cadover to his goal, or anything like it. But if her breath held—and she was pretty fit, thank goodness—she could still be in at the death.

At the death. . . . She frowned as she ran. One was never out of the shadow of the lethal in this queer nightmare into which her descent upon the Da Vinci Gallery had caught her up. And had caught John up too. . . . She increased her pace. A baby rabbit scurried ahead of her. And from in front she heard a rapid succession of sharp reports. It was the sound that she had been idiotic enough to suggest might be blasting.

The ploughland was behind her and the gradient rose steeply beneath her feet. Something was badly wrong; her running was poor and she felt oddly unsteady on her legs. For a moment she supposed furiously that she was overwrought; that the blonde was going hysterical in the rack. Then she realised that it was her shoes. What one naturally puts on to be chummy with Mervyn Twist is quite unsuitable for cross-country running. She kicked them off and felt better; her turn of speed improved. A cow was staring at her over a fence. It wasn't only a matter of shoes. She was wildly unsuitably dressed. Even a cow would laugh.

But she had made it. The path was converging upon the lip of the quarry on her left; and on her right was the very brow of the hill, with beyond it a valley still obscured in mist. A moment later she realised that Cadover could not have done better than positively recommend to her the path she had taken. Of whatever was happening or about to happen, this eminence gave her a superb view. But the quarry dropped sheer at her feet, cutting her off from participation in the action as completely as the invisible screen between a cinema audience and the violent world of shadows before it. She must be a spectator merely.

Almost immediately below her was the furniture van, like a black bug at bay during the close of an obscure insectile tragedy. Some confused conception of what constituted a position of strength appeared to have brought it there. It had its back to the wall—to the tremendous wall constituted by the perpendicular face of the quarry on the top of which Judith now stood. On either side of it was a litter of boulders, and among these there crouched the dark figures of three men. Occasionally a man moved an arm; there was a small spurt of fire, a drift of smoke, and a report that echoed sharply back from the great concave of living rock behind.

The quarry was semi-circular in form; a broad, rough track entered it at one end, curved to where the van stood, and then curved again to find its way out at the other. At each end of the track stood a car: to Judith's left was the green Humber; to her right, a large, black saloon with its bonnet hidden from view. And from behind both cars came the same little spurts of fire, the same reports—first sharp and then muted in echo within echo. There could be no doubt of it; she was watching a gun battle.

And suddenly she saw Cherry. He was standing with another man close by the black car, protected by an outcrop of rock. The two seemed to have paused in the battle to argue. Almost in the same instant that Judith spotted them, the second man turned and ran—ran headlong for the Humber. She realised that it must be Zhitkov—whose voice she had heard, but whom she had never seen. Zhitkov ran; he was shouting to his own people; perhaps he was appealing for some sort of covering fire. He had gone half the distance when Cherry whipped out a revolver and shot him in the back. He threw up his arms and Judith could see him scream. But before the sound reached her ears he was sprawled motionless on his face.

There were shouts of anger, fear, surprise. The spurts of flame changed direction. War had broken out between the two cars. But each continued its war with the van. The whole scene was like an allegory of the senseless history of human violence. Judith wondered what had become of Cadover, but even as this question entered her head she heard a single shrill blast on a whistle and saw the middle distance transform itself into an almost solid semi-circle of advancing police. Something drew her eye down again to the van. One of the men defending it had fallen back across a pile of stones. His face, covered with blood, stared up at her fixedly and meaninglessly. But it was not this that had attracted her attention. Among the little spurts of flame she had distinguished something different and even more sinister. Somewhere under the furniture van there was a red, angry glow, and even as she looked at this it grew, and sent up first one and then another licking tongue of fire. She cried out in horror, remembering the nameless police-station where there had enacted itself in her head just such a ghastly fantasy as was actually before her now. The flames clutched, spread, soared. There were double doors at the back of the van, and now she could see that they were being violently shaken. She cried out she didn't know what—her husband's name, an appeal for help—and dropped on her hands and knees at the edge of the quarry. There must be some way of getting down. . . .

She felt a hand on her shoulder; a mild voice uttered an indistinguishable but curiously authoritative dissuasive word; with eyes only for the horror below, she was aware of the presence beside her of some elderly man who appeared to have sprung from nowhere. "Revolvers," he said with disapproval. "Dangerous without being useful."

"John . . . my husband—he's in the van . . . the doors——"

The elderly man dropped flat on the lip of the quarry, and Judith suddenly saw that he was armed with a rifle. "Sort of bolt-affair at the top," he said. "Tricky." For two, three—perhaps five—seconds he became absolutely immobile, as if transformed into stone. Then he fired. The report mingled with a sharp clang of metal down below. The doors of the van flew open, and a man leapt out and flung himself upon one of the two remaining defenders. They rolled over and over in a cloud of dust—and then policemen were all around them. And the van had gone up like a torch. . . .

Judith gave either a gasp, or a sob, and turned round. The elderly marksman had risen and was placidly dusting down an antique knickerbocker-suit. "Reliable weapon, that," he said casually. "Took me a long way at Bisley once. . . . Morning, m'dear."

"You!" Judith stared at the Duke of Horton with rounded eyes. "How ever did *you* get here?"

The Duke looked surprised. "Odd question, 'pon my soul. Don't you know that you're on Horton Hill? Turn round. . . . Nice view, although I say it myself."

Judith turned. The mist had cleared from the broad,

shallow valley beneath them. And there, beyond a wisp of blue-grey smoke from the hamlet of Scamnum Ducis, beyond a stretch of park and a long vista of formal gardens, beyond its ornamental waters and above its marshalled terraces, gleaming in the low October sunlight like some pristine toy from a transcendental toy-shop, was all the serene, severe magnificence of Scamnum Court.

14

"Spot more coffee?" The Duke of Horton fussed amiably about his breakfast-room. Anne, he explained, was so excited that she would be down before nine o'clock—an unprecedented event. Meantime, he was concerned himself to do all honour to his guests. Judith gathered that it was not easy to set a decent breakfast before them. The Government denied the proprietor of Scamnum Court either the butter from his own famous Jerseys or the bacon from his scarcely less celebrated Large Blacks. *This* butter was national butter, and *this* bacon was national bacon. Judith might put tooth to them if she could. The Duke seemed so sure of his facts that Judith concluded it would be untactful to question them. And this seemed to be the opinion, too, of the Duke's butler, Bagot, who was himself presiding over breakfast in honour of this sensational occasion, and who served Judith with a further rasher of incomparable bacon while studiously preserving an expression of abasement and shame.

"But at least the marmalade is from our own oranges." The Duke brightened as this struck him. "A man should always insist on his own oranges in the marmalade. Madness to do anything else." He had drifted over to one of the lofty windows and was peering out. "Quite like a meet of the Horton—eh?" The long line of powerful police cars parked round the Great Court clearly intrigued him immensely, for he made this drift to the window every five minutes. "One of those fellows promised to show me how that walkie-talkie business works. Good name—what? Yankee, no doubt. Capital at names, the Yanks. But can't raise hogs."

Judith, while dutifully listening, let her glance stray to the other end of the long table, where John and Cadover were absorbedly comparing notes. They were like two small boys, happy over a puzzle. She found herself hoping, for their sake, that it would come out nicely. At the same time, her own indifference to it was complete. She felt—she acknowledged to herself—like a mother who has watched her small son's first rugger-match. It was necessary to be politely interested in the result, but all she really had room for was immense relief and happiness. Her glance went back to the Duke and followed him to the window once more. A break-down lorry had appeared in the Great Court, towing in the blackened shell of the burnt-out van. . . .

The Duke had turned from the window and walked over to the fireplace. He stood facing the warm glow, his eyes directed to the mantelpiece. And Judith saw that he had perched there George Stubbs's painting of his great-grandfather, seated in a curricle drawn by Goldfish and Silverfish, with his favourite groom, Morgan, holding Silverfish's head, and betraying, perhaps, the satisfied consciousness that here, celebrated by the latest fashionable painter, was an equipage not easily to be overgone even by so formidable a rival as his Grace of Richmond. . . . The Duke was thus regarding his Stubbs extremely contentedly—nevertheless Judith felt compunction for her own happiness as soon as her eye fell on him. He turned, glanced at her, and saw the state of the case in an instant. Crossing the room, he patted her on the head as if she were a small child. "M'dear," he said, "it's a great pity that picture has gone up in smoke, of course. But a live man is a lot more wonderful than any number of queer fish on a canvas." He wandered round the table and brought her a jar of honey. "Come to think of it, we've had our fill of queer fish in this affair." He chuckled. "Can't make head or tail of them myself, and I think it's time we had an explanation. That fellow, Cadover, is your husband's Number Two?"

"Yes."

"Asked me if I was an ichthyologist when I told him about the Aquarium. Clever of him—eh? Good joke. And now let's tackle both of them."

Appleby in his turn had gone to stare out of the window. He still looked anxious, Judith thought—but apart from that his night's adventures appeared to have left no mark on him. "Clear the thing up?" he said in reply to the Duke. "Yes, I think we're in a position to do that in no time. Shall I fire away?"

The Duke gave another serene glance at the Stubbs, and then nodded to Appleby. "Yes, my dear fellow, please do. If you've had a tolerably decent breakfast, that is to say."

"I've had a capital breakfast, thank you."

And Appleby sat back and explained.

"In puzzles of this sort it's not always the conscious mind, if you ask me, that works most rapidly and efficiently towards a solution. We know very well in the police that successful detection is often a matter more of intuition than of anything else. That simply means that the unconscious mind is making all the pace. And occasionally, of course, it throws us out hints. Cadover's did that on an occasion you already know of, when he talked about Limbert's death in terms of a superficial picture with something quite different beneath the surface. By that time, you remember, he had heard of the disappearance of the Aquarium—and in the depths of his mind he no doubt knew at once that the Aquarium was a famous picture that would need disguising, and not just an ichthyologist's tank."

Judith stretched herself lazily. She was beginning to feel beautifully sleepy. "I don't believe a word of it."

Her husband smiled. "The particular instance may be far-fetched, but the general proposition is sound enough. And one consequence is this: when you find yourself saying, or even thinking, something quite unusually vague and casual, listen in hard. After dinner last night, I made just such a remark about what we then believed to be Gavin Limbert's last painting. Do you remember? I was being thoroughly philistine, and suggesting that the picture was so meaningless that you might give it pretty well any fancy name you chose. And I suggested a couple of examples. One of them was *Project for a New Satellite Town*. Well now, that was a quite wonderful instance of what they call parapsychology. Because, you see, that was pretty well what the painting is. The thing came to me, I may say, in the darkness of that van. I *saw* the painting again with a sort of hallucinatory vividness—and in a flash I realised that it tallied with something very secret indeed that I'd been given a glimpse of some weeks ago. Limbert's supposed *chef-d'œuvre* was nothing more or less than a large-scale, very detailed plan of Waterbath."

"Waterbath!" Surprise brought Judith abruptly to her feet. "Oh, what an ass I've been! And Waterbath *is* a small new town. But of course, as everyone knows, it is something else as well."

Her husband looked at her sharply. "Just what do you mean by that?"

"I actually overheard Zhitkov and Cherry mention Waterbath. But because of some nonsense old Lady Clancarron had talked about baths, and because I was in a bit of a state, I got it the wrong way round. And rubbish about the bath water has been haunting me ever since. The unconscious mind again, no doubt."

"Demonstrably so. And now, begin at Waterbath. The mere detailed lay-out of the Research Station could be so informative that it is among the country's top secrets at this very moment. Only yesterday, Cadover was telling me about a scare there—a tale of small boys having managed to take photographs of bits and pieces of it. But the man who, you say, was called Crabbe, had more than that. On the night of Monday, the 22nd of October, he was in the Thomas Carlyle, waiting to hand over a complete set of plans of Wa-

239

terbath to a fellow-spy—none other than our friend Zhitkov. But Crabbe was being trailed by a rival organisation, which we may call Cherry's. And Zhitkov didn't come.

"Crabbe, I don't doubt, had been forbidden to contact Zhitkov in his studio. He hung about the club for a bit, happened to run into Limbert, who was an old school-fellow, and learnt that he had the flat immediately above Zhitkov's in Gas Street—which was no distance away. When Cherry and his friends arrived, Crabbe realised that his position was desperate, decided to contact Zhitkov at all costs, and headed for his studio. But Zhitkov, I imagine, wasn't one for courting danger, and had pretty well barricaded himself in. And now Crabbe's pursuers were on top of him; things looked so ugly that he took the first course to enter his head; he dashed upstairs to find shelter with Limbert. Limbert's studio was open and empty—Limbert, in point of fact, being upstairs with Miss Arrow—and Crabbe entered and secured the door. Probably he hoped to have given Cherry the slip altogether, and we can't tell just when he discovered that this wasn't so. For now an odd factor came into play. The police arrived in force to raid the Thomas Carlyle, and as a result the whole Gas Street set-up went into a sort of freeze. Zhitkov, who was a poor sort of creature, was cowering in his room; Crabbe had taken refuge in a strange, empty studio; Cherry and his confederates were lurking in force— and prepared to go to any lengths to get what they wanted.

"And this is the point at which I begin to admire Crabbe—to see him as a good man of his kind. He doesn't see himself as very likely to get out of his fix

240

alive, but he's not going to be beaten, all the same. He's the sort of spy, we must suppose, who is supported through danger by some strong political passion—not, like Zhitkov and Cherry, of the purely venal kind. He knows that if Cherry breaks in he will be killed, and the whole studio ransacked for the plans he is carrying. Well, perhaps he's a bit of a reading man; perhaps he remembers Poe's *Purloined Letter*. Certainly he has once been a bit of a painting man; that was what had once got him friendly with Limbert. His eye falls on a large blank canvas, and a brilliant idea comes to him. Transpose the stolen plans to *that*, preserving some approximation to Limbert's authentic abstract designs, and leave the result bang in the middle of the studio. Ten to one, the searchers simply won't glance at it.

"So that is what our resourceful friend addresses himself to. Unfortunately, as well as being resourceful, he is utterly ruthless. When Limbert pops in unexpectedly through a window, Crabbe simply takes him by surprise and shoots him dead at point-blank range. For this is a big thing, you see; and one can't even trust an old school pal.

"Crabbe now has some hope of getting clear, since there is this new and unsuspected factor of the fire-escape. But it is a slender chance, and he decides to carry on with his plan. So he closes and bolts the shutters, and then finishes his picture. It won't be much good, of course, if his friends don't know about it. But there is a telephone in the studio; Zhitkov is on the telephone too; Crabbe simply rings him up and explains. Zhitkov, still hiding in a funk in his own room, now knows how to find out all about Waterbath when opportunity comes. And then Crabbe finishes his painting. It has involved—as I noticed when I first set eyes on it—the working in of a great many intricate forms—Waterbath is an intricate sort of place—but he has done the whole thing with a rapid touch, giving some impression of an excited painter working as fast as he can in a free, bold technique. Crabbe burns the plans, and turns to give the thing a few final disguising touches. This is the point at which Mary Arrow appears outside the window and has her private view. She realises that the man before the easel is not her lover; she gives a scream; Crabbe pitches away his brushes and turns round in alarm; by this time the police have taken their departure, Cherry has got hold of a key from Boxer's room, and Crabbe's enemies are upon him just when he is caught off his guard from that direction. They kill him, search the studio, find nothing, and presently depart, taking Crabbe's body with them. Limbert's body they don't bother about, simply leaving beside it the pistol with which Crabbe had shot him. And now Zhitkov plucks up courage to make an appearance—presumably, as later, with some notion of a parley and a bargain. They slug him and pitch him back into his studio. And I think they probably slug Mary Arrow too. And that concludes the events of the night of October the 22nd in Gas Street."

Appleby paused to fill his pipe. "There is a certain intricacy about all this," he said. "But I hope I make myself clear so far."

The Duke of Horton, who was once more in communion with Goldfish and Silverfish, nodded amiably. "Capital power of exposition, my dear fellow. Would do well in the Lords."

"And now consider the position next morning. The door of Limbert's flat had, of course, secured itself when Cherry and his friends left. Zhitkov's best plan, when he again became an effective agent, would have been to break in and grab the picture straight away. But his nerve failed him there, and he probably reckoned that he could come by the thing in some more or less regular way quite soon. So he went to the police, Limbert's body was found, and we reach the point at which we make contact with the affair ourselves.

"It was an odd situation. Consider in turn all the parties concerned. Limbert and Crabbe were dead. Cherry knew nothing, except that he had been baffled in some way; his guess was that Crabbe had simply destroyed the plans without anybody benefiting; but he couldn't be certain, and he was still on the prowl. Zhitkov knew that what he wanted was spread broad over a canvas in the studio above his head. Mary Arrow, who had gone to earth with a lost memory, knew that the work on that canvas was by some sort of impostor. But *none* of them then knew about the really queer thing: that this canvas had first been used three hundred years ago by Jan Vermeer of Delft. *That* knowledge was confined to the gang—represented, for us, by old Moe Steptoe—who had originally made away with both the Vermeer and the Stubbs from this house. And, conversely, Steptoe and his friends had no idea that the canvas now showed anything other or more than an abstract composition by Gavin Limbert. In other words, the canvas had a completely different significance and value for two groups of criminals, and neither had any notion of the

243

existence of the other. A certain amount of bewilderment was bound to be the result.

"And now Braunkopf came along, secured all Limbert's work from his executors, and opened his exhibition at the Da Vinci. Zhitkov was uneasy: probably his whole unlikely story was being questioned by people higher up in his own organisation; and before the exhibition opened he tried, it seems, to get the picture photographed. A glance at that would probably convince his bosses that here really was Waterbath, and they would at once buy the painting. Steptoe's people got wind of this, mistakenly supposed that it was the police who were making inquiries, and were confirmed in that view when I happened to drop into the Da Vinci myself. So they took a chance, and recovered the picture there and then. It so happened that I gave Zhitkov his first news of its disappearance from the Da Vinci. Naturally, he was startled and upset. He must have suspected that Cherry had got ahead of him after all. But what, he must have asked himself, if that wasn't so? Nobody could really want to steal a Limbert. Was there any other explanation? Perhaps he had been about when Steptoe paid that visit to Limbert, and knew about the sort of racket he was mixed up with. Certainly by yesterday evening he had worked his way to the truth. And his friends in the green Humber were preparing to pounce on old Moe's junk shop, when old Moe's friends nipped in and carried the Vermeer off in their van—and myself as well. But meanwhile Zhitkov had been feeling nervous about Cherry; had decided to try coming to terms with him; had made, and then failed to keep, an appointment at the Thomas Carlyle; and in the end had gone through the interview that Judith overheard. And that is pretty nearly the end of the story."

Appleby had got to his feet and was pacing about the room. He seemed to have caught from the Duke an urge to take intermittent glances through the window. For a moment he was silent and preoccupied. Then he continued his recital.

"Or say that it is the beginning of the final chase. The van is making for some confederate who keeps an aeroplane near Fawley. The men with it are uneasy, for the operation is an emergency one, and they have got away only after fighting off an unknown stranger—myself—in the darkness of Steptoe's shop. They must be wondering just where they stand, and it can't be long before they see that they are being trailed. Behind them, as we know, are Zhitkov's folk in the Humber, and a spy of Cherry's on a motorbike. Their first thought will be that here are the police. But soon they must have doubts about that. The police wouldn't trail them indefinitely; they would simply pull them up short. They can't make it out. And so begins with them the panic that brings the van eventually to bay in that quarry. Meanwhile Cherry's spy has contacted his chief, and Cherry and Zhitkov, having patched up an agreement, hurtle across country to be in at the kill. And there was quite a lot of killing."

"There might have been even more." Judith, who had joined the Duke by the fireplace, frowned into the flames. "But, John, haven't you missed something out? What about Hildebert Braunkopf and his Baby Austin?"

"As to that, he must tell you himself." Appleby,

still at the window, tapped the glass. "For here he is. And bringing something to the Duke."

"Bringing *me* something?" The Duke of Horton swung round. "You can't mean——"

Appleby chuckled—and only Judith knew what vast relief there was in the sound. "Certainly. The *chef-d'œuvre* of Gavin Limbert, to be hung in the picture gallery of Scamnum Court. What more could a respectable picture-dealer desire?"

They had all crowded to the window. And there, sure enough, was Mr Hildebert Braunkopf or Brown, driving sedately past the long row of police cars in an ancient Austin Seven. And there was a large parcel cocked in the back.

It was half an hour later. They were standing in the picture gallery before an empty space on the wall. Near at hand, under the big Velasquez, and leaning against a magnificent Spanish chest, was the ambiguous work of art which the ingenuity of Mr Braunkopf had christened The Fifth and Sixth Days of Creation. The Duke of Horton gave it a long look. "We'll hang it," he said.

"Hang it!" Cadover was scandalised. "Does your Grace realise——"

"We'll hang it for five minutes. I'm always on the look-out, you know, for a bit of history to add to Scamnum. The occasion when we hung the country's top secret between Frans Hals's Fishwife and Hobbema's Fountain in a Glade will be distinctly one of them. Bagot, fetch a step-ladder."

Cadover looked doubtfully at his chief and saw that the point was to be conceded. "If that's to be the way of it," he said handsomely, "I hope your Grace will let me lend a hand. Later, of course, it must be taken away under escort, and whoever does the cleaning for you will be under the supervision of the police."

"To be sure, my dear fellow." The Duke turned to Appleby. "I don't quite understand about Brown."

"Last night he must have decided to investigate Steptoe on his own. He is, one must remember, a very enterprising man."

"Certainly he is. Tried to sell me all those dam' Limberts, lock, stock and barrel. Sorry, m'dear."

"And not having one of his three four big new Daimler cars precisely to hand, he got out his little Austin. When the procession started, he followed along. I could see out of the back of the van, you know, and after a while I recognised him. I'd found the picture—the hunt through the van took me about half-an-hour—and made certain preparations. I didn't like the look of the Humber, or of the motor-cyclist either. But I decided that, if I got the opportunity, I'd take a chance and trust Brown. A big military convoy did the trick; the procession got out of order for a time, and there was the Austin, crawling along directly behind me. So I crossed my fingers and tumbled the picture out."

"Tumbled the picture out? But I thought——"

"The position was much as it had been in this gallery at the time of the theft. What was available to me was a long, narrow slit which it would just go through." Appleby paused. "By the way, I put a message on the wrapping." He bent down. "And here it is. I don't doubt that when Brown has had breakfast he will modestly call your attention to it. I'm afraid I require your indemnity. But I thought it might just turn the scale." He held up a piece of stout paper and they read:

WITH CARE
This package contains
A VALUABLE PAINTING
Stolen by thieves and now
Recovered by a police officer
Who has been forced to abandon it during a
chase.
It is the property of
THE DUKE OF HORTON, K.G.
of Scamnum Court
Who on the return of his property will be
MOST GRATEFUL
and pay
£500 REWARD